Abram Bogart Burrell

Reminiscences of George La Bar

the centenarian of Monroe County, Pa., who is still living in his 107th year!

And incidents in the early settlement of the Pennsylvania side of the river

valley, from Easton to Bushkill

Abram Bogart Burrell

Reminiscences of George La Bar
*the centenarian of Monroe County, Pa., who is still living in his 107th year! And
incidents in the early settlement of the Pennsylvania side of the river valley, from
Easton to Bushkill*

ISBN/EAN: 9783337369347

Printed in Europe, USA, Canada, Australia, Japan

Cover: Foto ©Andreas Hilbeck / pixelio.de

More available books at **www.hansebooks.com**

OF

GEORGE LA BAR,

THE

CENTENARIAN OF MONROE COUNTY, PA.,

WHO IS STILL LIVING IN HIS 107TH YEAR!

AND INCIDENTS IN THE EARLY SETTLEMENT OF THE
PENNSYLVANIA SIDE OF THE RIVER VALLEY,
FROM EASTON TO BUSHKILL.

BY A. B. BURRELL.

With a Portrait.

PHILADELPHIA:
CLAXTON, REMSEN & HAFFELFINGER,
819 & 821 MARKET STREET.
1870.

STEREOTYPED BY J. FAGAN & SON.   PRINTED BY MOORE BROS.

TO THE

"OLD FOLKS"

OF NORTHAMPTON AND MONROE,

WHO BEGAN LIFE IN THE PAST CENTURY,

AND WHO ARE WITH US TO-DAY,

𝔗𝔥𝔦𝔰 𝔏𝔦𝔱𝔱𝔩𝔢 𝔙𝔬𝔩𝔲𝔪𝔢

IS RESPECTFULLY DEDICATED BY

THE AUTHOR.

PREFACE

THIS little volume has been drawn together by frequent conversations with the aged pilgrim with whom those talks were had. His mind operates slowly, and in its operations it often slides out of the channel upon which it first sets out, upon thoughts or topics suggested as he goes along. For this reason the book has been divided into chapters, with dates somewhat mixed.

As the old blood becomes sluggish in its flow through the system, so, too, the mind, in sympathy with the body, loses its earlier elasticity, although, like the blood, it still exercises its wonted purpose. And this arrangement of Nature is well, for thus the body and the mind work in unison to the end, and that calmness which prepares for the final separation of body and soul, comes gently, unconsciously on, loosing the hold to earth, and preparing for heaven. Oh, how beautiful is this calm, yet cheerful spirit of the old! How it attracts and makes us happy to be near such, creating a reverential feeling within us, that makes us forget the toils of life to look complacently on the loosing of the " silver cord," and the opening to the beautiful land Beulah!

The historic part of this volume is, of course, fragmentary, touching here and there the early settlement of the Pennsylvania side of the river valley reaching from Easton to Bushkill. The picture of to-day is in wide contrast with that of one hundred and seven years ago. Then, the Indians claimed all this valley region, and the white settlements only here and there showed a clearing, and the struggle for the mastery had not closed. Now, the red men are all gone, and the evidences of the superiority of our race are shown on every hand, proving that the Supreme Being had reserved this country for the enterprise and development of a new people and a new dispensation.

A. B. B.

Delaware Water Gap, Pa.

CONTENTS

CHAPTER IX.

REMINISCENCES

OF

GEORGE LA BAR.

CHAPTER I.

INTRODUCTORY.

In this frail tenement shall we
Elude its thousand foes,
And, zigzag, journey till we see
A century round us close?

AMONG the millions who inhabit this earth
to-day, how rare it is to find a centenarian!
Surrounded as we are by ten thousand hidden by-ways, which terminate in death, it is difficult to reach even the "threescore and ten," to which all have a right. I say "right," because, aside from accidents, our ignorance or our follies make us our own suicides — if we escape the blunders of our parents — while a good Providence is censured for the shortened life-term. To see five score is almost

9

a miracle; and when we find a rare old relic of
one hundred and six years, we may well become
interested in him, and anxiously ask what have
been his tastes and his habits?

Beholding that human form, which bears the
burden of over a century, no one would ask to
have his life so lengthened out; and yet few are
they who have lived so long as they would
wish. Weakened, tremulous old age has nothing in it to invite us to share and to bear the
same; and, with the fullest assurance of a blessed
immortality, there is something so sad, so re-
pulsive in death, that, palsied and wrinkled, we
still cling to life, ask for another and yet an-.
other day, until, pushed off the stage of existence, we are gathered to our fathers.

One hundred and six years back through the
buried past, and what changes, what wonders we
reach beyond! What vast, what mighty revelations have been unfolded during those years!
What tornadoes of thought and action have
swept over nations and societies, building up
and tearing down, leaving footprints to live in
history so long as time shall be! What mira-
cles of science and civilization! What strides
of human progress and development!

And all this measured by a life whose sands
are not exhausted! Can we still talk with one
who heard the booming cannons of the Revolution, and who participated in the rejoicings after

that trying war was over? Can we shake hands
with one who saw the stately Washington?
Yes, he lives, a marvelous volume, a living
record of one hundred and six years! Eighteen such lives would reach back to the time
of Christ. Only eighteen times for the tale to
be handed down from sire to son to reach
through the dim distance! Eighteen generations instead of an average of fifty-seven!

CHAPTER II.

PERSECUTION.

The Indian war-whoop echoed round
  The place where he was born;
They claimed it as their hunting-ground,
  And theirs to grow their corn:
The settlers' huts were rough and rude,
  And few and far between,
Scarce broken Nature's solitude,
  A weird, foreboding scene.

GEORGE LA BAR, the subject of this
sketch, was born in the autumn of 1763,
in Mount Bethel, Northampton County, Pennsylvania, about half-way between Slateford and
Portland, and half a mile from that road, over-
looking the Delaware River, and is, therefore,
in his one hundred and seventh year.

His grandfather came to this country from
France, about the year 1730, on account of religious persecution. It was persecution that
had driven the Pilgrim Fathers to the wilds of
America many years before, and there were
many to follow still.

It was Jehovah's gracious plan
To open here a home for man,
Where persecution could not bind
The faithful heart and earnest mind;
And here he came, content to dare
All other evils and to bear,

If pleading conscience could be free
To worship with soul-liberty.

Just before and immediately after 1730, there was a new impetus given to immigration to Penn's Colony. They came from Germany, France, Ireland, England, and other countries; but nearly all were Dissenters, Protestants, under various denominational names.

A certain kind of Protestantism was protected in England, but all forms of vital, earnest, unselfish religion were kept outside the pale of humanity, not only there, but in all Catholic countries throughout the Old World; and to teach and to live the religion of Christ was to open the door to persecution, torture, and death, alike from pagan and Catholic.

The history of all Catholic countries has been a history written in blood. Looking into the catacombs of Spain, but lately opened to the gaze of the outside world, we see but a slaughter which has had its counterpart in many, many places of like faith and practice! Oh, what suffering has been endured for the cause of Christ! How comparatively easy is the path of the devoted follower of the meek and lowly Jesus in this nineteenth century, to that of all previous years! The light long prayed for and long waited, has dawned at last; and almost everywhere throughout the habitable globe, man can worship the true God according to the dictates of his own conscience. Glad millennium! how should every Christian heart rejoice over the day-star of promise realized! The right has triumphed in this nineteenth century, and ignorance and bigotry and superstition have fallen to rise no more. The glorious light of the Bible has penetrated the thick darkness of other days, and the Sun of Righteousness beams effulgently upon us despite centuries of opposition. God rules, and the powers of darkness must succumb.

CHAPTER III.

EARLY BOUNDARIES.

Honest heart and iron will
Danger cannot thwart or thrill;
Clouds may settle thick as night,
Dare and do will bring the light.

NOW let us turn to Pennsylvania at the time Mr. La Bar was born, and a few years previous to that time. The three original counties of Chester, Bucks, and Philadelphia, formed by William Penn in 1682, had been increased by only four more, Lancaster, York, Northampton, and Berks. Northampton was formed from Bucks in 1752, and is, therefore, but eleven years older than La Bar. At this time the western boundary of the Colony, or counties, was little more than a myth, and full of dissatisfaction and trouble to the white settlers, as well as to the Indians. The Great Indian Walk, which took place just twenty-six years before 1763, was the first great source of contention and bloodshed to the settlers of the Forks region. Previous to that Walk the settlers of Penn's Colony had dwelt together in peace with the Indians. The kindness of Penn created a corresponding spirit in them, which lasted through many years; but after the father of the Colony was gone, the white man's treachery revealed itself, stirred up the savage nature of the red man, and many an innocent mother and child paid the penalty with their lives.

The original Forks was all the known region of country reaching from the mouth of the Lehigh, bounded on the east by the Delaware River, and north and west by the Kittatinny Mountain, and extending beyond this mountain into the unknown west as far as any settler might dare to go. Easton, though laid out for a town as early as 1737, was but little settled upon until after 1752, when Northampton, or the Forks, had been constituted a county. From that time up to 1761 it was a favorite place for holding Indian councils with their chiefs and head warriors, and it was not uncommon to see from two hundred to five hundred Indians present on such occasions with the white officials of the province and of other colonies.

William Parsons, an officer of the province, was sent to East Town, or Easton, in the fall of 1753. He gives us a lengthy letter, under that date, of the prospect of a town at that place. He fears a rival in Bethlehem, and also across the river, where Phillipsburg now stands. He fears, too, that the one hundred acres of land, which lie surrounded by hills, will not afford room enough for much of a town; but he eulogizes the water-power, and the navigation of the Delaware and the Lehigh " for small craft, for several miles." He says there is no clay for brick, which might be a drawback also. At this time there were eleven families in Easton, all of whom proposed to stay there through the winter.

In 1758 there was not a wagon in Easton township, and only four draught and five pack horses. In Mount Bethel township there were nine wagons, twenty-four draught and eleven pack horses.

Position of Troops in Northampton County, 1758.

Captain Van Etten, at Minisink (Bush Kill), a lieutenant, and	30 men.
Captain Craig, at Fort Hamilton (Stroudsburg) .	41 "
Lieutenant Wetherhold, at Brodhead's . .	26 "
Ensign Sterling, at Wind Gap, Teel's House .	11 "

Captain Orndt, at Fort Norris (between Wind
    Gap and Bossard's) . . . .   50 men.
Captain Wayne, at Fort Allen . . . 50 "
A sergeant at Uplinger's, and . . .   5 "
An ensign of Wetherhold's, at Donker's Mills   15 "
A lieutenant in Allen township, and . . . 15 "
Captain Foulk, at the new fort, not named, be-
    tween Fort Allen and Fort Lebanon . . 63 "
Captain Trexler (has posted himself, contrary to
    orders, within the mountains) . . . . 53 "
Captain Martin (in the settlement above Easton) . 30 "
                                          ——
                                       389 "

A squad of men was usually kept at Philip
Bossard's, about six miles from Fort Hamilton.
It was not far from Bossard's that Peter Hess,
Nicholas Coleman, and one Gottlieb were killed
in 1756 by a party of Indians under Teedyuscung. Henry Hess, a son of Peter, was carried off by them, and returned, after an absence
of several months.

In 1757, Philip Bossard was driven away from
his plantation, with all his neighbors, and took
refuge below the mountain. They petitioned
the Governor for troops, and they were sent.

On the 21st of June, 1757, Captain Van
Etten sent a guard of a corporal and ten men
to escort Samuel Depui's wife, who was sick,
to a doctor at Bethlehem.

The chief Teedyuscung was prominent at this
time, and he took active part in the councils.
He exhibited a native eloquence in his speeches,

2

which told upon his hearers, without education
or the rules of oratory. He professed to be the
leader of the Lenapes, and contended for their
rights, against other tribes, and against the in-
trusion of the whites. He had been baptized
into the Moravian faith, at Bethlehem; but
whether his conversion was genuine, many
have serious doubts to-day. But, if he was
sincere in his belief that his people had wrongs
which should be redressed, he certainly had the
right to contend for justice, even though it led
through blood. He seems to have lived for
some time somewhere near where Stroudsburg
now stands.

In 1763 the Indians made the last desperate
attempt to drive the white settlers from the
valley below the Blue Ridge, and from Water
Gap to Bethlehem many families were butchered by the savages pouring over the mountains from the north. Many of the whites
escaped across the Delaware, as they had frequently done before. Teedyuscung was the
leader of the terrible raid. He, at last, came
to a violent death by the hands of men of his
own race at Wilkesbarre.

At the very time of this fearful sweep of carnage and death, George was born; but, in their
hurry to reach the more populous settlements
further toward the Lehigh, the Indians left his
father's hut unmolested, and there the family

remained through all that terrible crisis, which
below them swept death and destruction to so
many. With such alarming scenes passing
before them, the parents of George might well
question the wisdom of their fathers, who had
left a land of boasted civilization to bear, with
their descendants, the terrors of a frontier life
among a race of men who could join in a mad
carnival and war-dance, with the bloody scalps
of their white victims dangling from their gir-
dles! But they were free from the thraldom
of European bigotry, and freemen in the sight
of God. It did not require much argument and
reasoning to satisfy themselves that it was
better to suffer all these perils and dangers
here, in a home of privation, and surrounded
by wild natives, than to be slaves, though in
the midst of luxury, but persecuted and fettered.

The grandfather La Bar — or Le Barre, as
the name was brought over the Atlantic, and
Lawar, as the Germans had it — came to this
wild, new country, expecting there would be
hardship, trial, and danger. But he knew all
this would not fetter his conscience, and it was
this liberty, above every other, that he sought.
For this he was willing to brave every other
difficulty. Of two evils he chose the least.

Two brothers came with him, and they landed
at Philadelphia. It took many weeks to cross
the ocean then, and who shall guess the tor-

nado of swelling thoughts that swept through
those brothers' breasts as, day after day, the distance grew greater and greater between them
and all the dear ones left behind? And then
the unknown future, to be spent in a far-off
country, and in an unknown spot! Ah, all this
needed nerve and courage.

> That trying scene of long ago,
> No pen or pencil now can show;
> 'T is through a glass we darkly see
> What men will suffer to be free!

CHAPTER IV.

THE ARRIVAL.

> "The New World"—'twas the proper name—
> They saw a wondrous change;
> Nothing like that from which they came—
> All, save the sky, was strange!

THE grandfather's name was Peter; the
brothers', Charles and Abraham. They
were young men, stout and large, full of daring, and bound on a bold enterprise, to do or
die. After spending a few days at the Philadelphia settlement, learning what could be
learned of the new country and its wild men,
they determined to follow up, up the Delaware
River, until they had passed the very frontier

of all white settlements, to plant themselves
among the aborigines of the land. In three
days they arrived at the Forks, or immediately
below, which was then the principal settlement.
Here they also stopped for a day or two. Just
in the Forks, between the Delaware and Lehigh
rivers, and where Easton now stands, was quite
an Indian village. It was an odd village of
odd citizens to the Frenchmen.

Continuing their journey through the wilderness, following Indian paths as best they
could, and always keeping in sight of the river,
at length they came in view of the Blue Ridge
barrier. There were some small settlements
back from the river, one near Martin's Creek,
one at Richmond, and at Williamsburg. But
these they passed round by following the river.
At this time there was no settlement above
Williamsburg, along the river, until Nicholas
Depui's, who was comfortably planted at what
is now Shawnee. The brothers supposed they
had passed beyond the very outskirts of civilization, and, after viewing the country between
the river and the mountain for a day or two,
they pitched upon a site for their cabin, about
three-quarters of a mile from the river, on a
somewhat elevated spot. The cabin was soon
erected. The natives were their only near
neighbors, and these they managed to make
their true friends by many little acts of kind-

ness. This friendship was of untold benefit to
the La Bar family in after days, when deception
and intrigue had roused the ire of the savages
to deeds of blood and death. Perhaps it is
hardly proper to call the Indians of Penn's
Colony "savages," for they were not really such
until after the noted Walk, by which means
they were deceived and cheated. But after
1737 they looked upon most of the whites as
enemies and intruders, and their tomahawks
were now used for a new purpose. Luckily for
the La Bars, they had ingratiated themselves
into the good graces of the Indians before the
great enmity was stirred up between the races.

The brothers mixed freely with the Indians,
without fear, and a mutual interest and welfare
existed between them. Their cabin-home and
its surroundings were in wide contrast with
their home in the country of their birth, and
which they had now turned their backs forever
upon; and many and trying were the difficulties under which they were placed; but they
were free to worship their God unmolested.
Their rude cabin, made of small logs and
mud, and covered with bark and split timber,
lapped together, was a home more to be desired by them than the more convenient home
of their fatherland. There they were cramped
and dwarfed in spirit, and looked upon themselves as less than serfs.

The wild man's fare was not more wild than their own; for their subsistence had to be drawn from the woods and river, until a patch could be cleared to grow their corn and beans. Oh, what will not man bear to be free? Immortal man, fettered and bound by man! He may be for a season; and thousands may pay the purchase-price with their lives for soul-liberty, but it must come, it has come!

It was a romantic picture — these three French brothers, Crusoe-like, cut off from civilization, living in a hunter's hut, and determined to make the wilderness their home. While one might be toasting the venison, and preparing the breakfast meal, another might be seen mending his leather breeches, and the other dressing up the flint of his gun, preparatory to the excursion for the day. A few camping articles had been brought with them; but none of these were more important than the mortar and pestle for pounding their corn, which they obtained of their red neighbors. They could not, at once, live on game alone; and the corn they got of the Indians was their only bread, which, to their appetites, sharpened by much exercise and exposure, was most palatable.

The first three months of their cabin-life were spent in explorations throughout the surrounding region; and they were not long in finding the Depui settlement, above them; and, though they were disappointed to find themselves not the farthest in the wilderness, yet they were glad to find a store of supplies so near.

The Indians inhabiting the Minisink region — which was the river valley between Delaware Water Gap and Carpenter's Point — were the Wolf, or Minsi, called by the English Monseys. They were a warlike tribe, strong friends while they were friends, but bloodthirsty when enemies. The name Delaware was given by the whites to all the tribes in the vicinity of the river, but they called themselves the Lenni Lenapes, or *original people.* They had long been warring with the Six Nations, and professed to have been victorious.

One of the first purchases by William Penn of land from the Indians was measured by walking, in which Penn took a *walking* part himself. He walked as they walked, slowly, stopping frequently to smoke and talk and to be refreshed. They were satisfied. The first line reached up the river to Trenton. When more land was wanted, Penn's agents flattered the Indians to consent to a day and a half's walk from the first tract. The deed was written and signed, with plenty of blank space to be filled up to suit an avaricious taste. Expert walkers were advertised for. An air-line path was cut out; and it is said a trial walk was experimented upon, in order to make a good thing of it; and all unknown to the Indians.

The Walk came off in the fall of 1737; and there was no stopping to smoke, to rest, or to be refreshed. It was walk, walk, walk, from sun to sun. The Pennites had found the very man for their purpose, Edward Marshall. Yeates and one Indian kept up with Marshall through the first day, and they reached the north side of the Blue Ridge, through the Wind Gap, at sunset. There was half a day to walk yet, and the Lehigh hills — the farthest point that the Indians had supposed the walk to extend — had been passed three hours before. They began to murmur at the cheat, and, when Marshall started next morning, he had to go alone. The country north of the Forks was the Indians' favorite ground. They feared it would now be lost; the whites wanted to reach around the Minisink.

At twelve o'clock, Marshall was at Pocono Point, now Tannersville. Taking advantage of the curve in the river, it was declared that the line strike the river at Lackawaxen. Thus the Minisink was swooped into the Penn Colony. From the point where Marshall ended his walk it took *four days to reach the river.* Had they aimed for the *nearest* point, they would have reached it at Water Gap in less than a day! But then it would not have taken in the coveted prize. The Indians were disappointed, chagrined, angry, and they were ready for retaliation. While they were friends the whites had taught the Indians the use of the firearms they had put in their hands, and now they were teaching them the science of deception and intrigue. The Indians were thus fully equipped to resent the injury and remember the insult.

The French language was very useful to the brothers in communicating their thoughts to one another, but with the Indians it was useless, and they set themselves to acquire this language. It would have been amusing could we have seen them trying, again and again, to draw out, by signs, the Indian names of gun, deer, fish, fire, water, etc., in order to make a start and catch the least hold of the language. But it is perseverance that conquers, and, at the close of the first year, they had acquired a tolerably fair idea of the Lenape language, and could converse quite freely with their red friends. They did not know they would soon be under the necessity of learning yet another tongue. But overcoming one difficulty enabled them the more easily to surmount the next, and nothing daunted their resolution.

CHAPTER V.

EARLY SETTLERS.

And still they come, an earnest band,
Believing this the Promised Land.

OTHER settlers followed rapidly into Hunter's settlement, principally from Germany, spreading out from the main clearings, until, at length, each of the brothers took German wives. It matters not if they popped the question at corn-huskings, at clearings, to the music of the sickle, or at the quilting; for the women were always present on all these occasions. Whatever the "bee," it came to be that they became married men, and their French was useless, unless to have a three-cornered chat about the merits or demerits of their *fraus*, when these rustic ladies were present. However hard it might be to unlearn the French, the German was now the lesson, for the women would have their own way even at that time.

Now the cabin is too small, and there must be a spreading out. Peter takes his Dutch teacher and pushes a little farther on, and bought a tract of land above the mountains of the Indians. Years after, he had to buy it again. This tract was southwest of where

Stroudsburg now stands, and adjoining a tract
Colonel Stroud purchased some time after.
Stroud was the founder of Stroudsburg. The
settlement of N. Depui, at Shawnee, was made
very much earlier. In fact, it is thought by
many historians that this was the very first
white settlement in the State. Penn's Colony
had been planted forty years before he knew
of this settlement; and when, in 1737, he sent
agents to look after the "squatter," Depui could
give no positive date of the first clearing. He
seemed to be on the right side of the Indians,
but when Penn's surveyor undertook to run
out the place, they advised him to "put up iron
string," which he did. The Depui settlers had
come across from Esopus; and thither they had
a good communication by what was called
the "Mine Road." They did not then know
whither the river led.

N. Depui—Depue or Depuy the name now
is — raised Colonel Stroud. It was not uncommon, at that early day, for immigrants to
this country to sell themselves, or their services, for a term of years, for their passage-
money; and this was done in the case of Stroud
to N. Depui, and for whom he worked until his
time was expired.

Stroud was a colonel in the Revolution, and
had command of Fort Penn, which was situated
just west of the "great wash" of the past year.

The old Indian fort was farther up, near the west end of the town, and was built around Peter La Bar's house.

The Colonel had made a good selection for operation, and immediately after the Revolution he became the greatest business-man north of the mountains, having a grist-mill, (the second in all this region, Depui's mill being oldest,) a store, tavern, and he had, sometimes, as many as twenty men felling trees and clearing up the land. There was a great deal of card-playing at this time, as there always is just after the toils and relaxations of war, and, on one occasion, the Colonel's choppers thought they would suspend work and take a quiet game. So they stationed two men up a tree, to watch for the "boss," and to give timely notice if he should be seen coming toward them. The sentinels became careless; the Colonel came up behind them, suspected the game, and ordered them down from the tree. They obeyed, and when they had reached the ground, he began to play cane upon their heads, at the same time telling them to "watch better next time."

In the early Indian wars there was a line of forts, or block-houses, in front, reaching from Weisport to N. Depui's, and the Governor sent Benjamin Franklin to pay off the soldiers stationed at the different forts, and to report as to the prospect of the country. He took observa-

tions, which were published. He stopped with
N. Depui, and while there, a young Brodhead,
son of Daniel, was "sparking" the old man's
daughter, and, as he was a frontier man, he
thought the Colony owed him services, as well
as the more idle soldiers. Franklin denied the
claim, saying it was unnecessary for a man to
stand guard over a woman who lived in a fort.
The Brodhead clearing was, at this time, about
one mile east of where Stroudsburg Depot now
stands, and on the old Smith place.

Speaking of the Depui place, it is a remarkable fact, for this country, that the old, old
homestead is still in the hands of a descendant
of the same name.

Peter La Bar, the Frenchman, cleared up a
good home, after many years of hard labor, and
raised a large family of children. He had seen
many trying times, and was often called upon
to assist those who came for refuge to his family in Fort Hamilton. He always stuck to the
homestead he had hewn out from the rough;
but the religion he had sacrificed so much for
at an earlier day, was sadly neglected. The
occasion to battle for religious liberty having
passed away, the value of the privilege seems
to have been forgotten. How is it some men
seem to live too long for their own good?
When men outlive their piety they live too long.

Whisky brought the fall. Stroudsburg had

its whisky-shop then, and Peter patronized that shop too well for his own good and the good of his family. His substance became scattered, his family broken up, and the end came. George remembers his old French grand-father distinctly. His intemperance brought on something like the palsy, and lying, half help-less, for some months, with a rope dangling from the beams above his head to help him to turn in his bed, he died when George was present. This lesson against intemperance he never forgot.

One of the French brothers, Charles, remained on the old cabin homestead in Mount Bethel, and the other, Abraham, planted himself above the Water Gap Notch, not far from the Water Gap Depot. Here he lived many years, also raising a large family. He cleared the islands just above the Gap, which, with the garden-flat around his house, made quite a snug farm. His islands are little more now than gravelly *bars*, the *la* (lay) part, which made the name, being *lain* somewhere farther down the Delaware.

Abraham La Bar first opened and walled up that noble old spring near the house of Samuel Williams in Dutotsburg, and which still flows to bless the human family, as well as other families.

Abraham La Bar, as well as some of his sons, had to carry his musket in one hand while go-ing to the spring after water with a pail in the other. The path was through a perfect thicket of laurel, hazel, and alder, that led to the spring, and there was no telling at what step an Indian might be met.

Abraham La Bar lived here in 1741, when the Governor sent Nicholas Scull up to look after the state of things in the Smithfields. The principal settlers in this vicinity, then, were N. Depui, Abraham Van Campen, Jacobus Kirkendall, Daniel Brodhead, and Jacob Kirkendall, and they had petitioned the Governor to send them help, as the Indians were retaliating on them for the wrong of the Indian Walk. It was in answer to this call that Scull was sent. He gave the Indians to understand that if they did not submit to the state of things, the Governor would call for their enemies, the Six Nations, to help him, and they would exterminate the Minisink Indians. They were alarmed, and promised to do better.

As late as 1763, we find the following petition laid before the Colonial Government by the inhabitants of Lower Smithfield:

"LOWER SMITHFIELD, NORTHAMPTON COUNTY, *1st September,* 1763.

"To the Honorable JAMES HAMILTON, Esq., Lieutenant-Governor and Commander-in-Chief of the Province of Pennsylvania:

"We, the within subscribers, inhabitants residing upon the frontiers of the Province of Pennsylvania, in the County of Northampton, do, from divers reasons, reports, and information, and from different accounts we have from the Ohio that the savages are committing their cruel barbarities, we have the greatest reason in life to expect those savage Indians will extend their cruel barbarities as far as our places. As we are in no order of defence, but lie entirely open to the mercy of those barbarous savage Indians, who delight in the shedding of innocent blood, and for the defence of any attempts which might be made of the like, a number of us have formed and enjoined ourselves under articles in an associated, independent company, as loyal subjects to our king and country, ready and willing to defend whatever attempts those barbarians might make upon our settlements; for which we have, thirty of us, unanimously chosen Mr. John Vancampen as captain, Mr. Joseph Wheeler lieutenant, and Cornelius Vancampen ensign. And your humble petitioners pray your Honor will be pleased to grant us your assistance in carrying out so loyal a design. And your petitioners will ever pray.

" BENJAMIN SHOEMAKER,	MICHAEL SLY,
ELIJAH SHOEMAKER,	BENJAMIN FOSTER,
WILLIAM SMITH,	BENJAMIN VANCAMPEN,
NICHOLAS DEPUI,	JONATHAN HUNLOCK,
JAMES HIGERMAN,	JOHN COUNTRYMAN,
BENJ. SHOEMAKER, JR.,	HENRY PENSIL,
MOSES SHOEMAKER,	CHARLES DELOY,
WILLIAM CLARK,	JOHN CHAMBERS,
LEONARD WESER,	BENJAMIN ONEY,
CHARLES HOLMES,	PETER HAINS,
JOHN CAMDEN,	ISAAC VANORMEN,
WILLIAM DEVORE,	WILLIAM CARREL,
BENJAMIN HAINS,	JOSEPH HAINS,
JOHN FISH,	JAMES ERREL,
SAMUEL HYNDY,	GARRET SHOEMAKER."

For the benefit of those whose tongue has never been muzzled by a king, we quote the

3

following. The Marshall mentioned was son of the Indian walker, who seems to have thought there was unfair dealing in it.

"EASTON, *July 27th,* 1757.

"We do certify that we heard William Marshall say the following words, or words to the same effect, viz.: That the Proprietors had wronged the Indians out of their lands; and that he would prove it; and that, in that respect, he abided by the Indians.

"DANIEL BRODHEAD,
EDWARD BIDDLE."

It was the original French brothers who first cut the road through the mountain gap which was afterward named Tat's Gap. It was a hard road, but it led in almost a direct line from the early cabin to Peter's place. The valley just north of the mountain was then named "Deer Park," but has since been known as Wolf Hollow and Poplar Valley. It looks, even yet, as though it might have been wolfish before it was settled as now. From the western ridge of this valley opens a grand view, of many miles' extent, reaching to the Pocono Mountains, and taking in Pocono Point, where Marshall ended his great walk.

CHAPTER VI.

THE ESTRANGEMENT.

No matter where or what it be,
'T is home where opens infancy.

IN such a pioneer home, surrounded by the stern realities of wilderness life, and a race of men more wild than nature itself, was the father of George reared to a life of fearless hardihood. At first, cut off almost entirely from the known world, inhabitants of the New, a kingdom of the patriarchal, like the early Jews, though much less numerous, they lived, struggled, reared families, spread out cultivated fields, made some little progress in civilization and in the art of living, grew old, and died.

George's father married, and moved to the south side of the mountain, and not far from the original cabin. He was a bold, impetuous, wicked man, though his wife was a religious woman. He cared little for that religion which had led his father and his uncles to brave so much before he was born. But he had seen his father show very little respect for the same, if he had not entirely lost all; and who shall not say that the father's unfaithfulness was much of the cause of the son's wickedness?

His name was George, also, and his rashness set the Indians against him. He was not in the least afraid of them, and any trick he could play upon them he enjoyed hugely, even though it might cost a poor Indian his life. He considered himself too smart to be beaten by a redskin, and to carry out his theory to perfection required no little tact and watchfulness on his own part. If a strange Indian should ask him for information on any subject, he would make it a point to give him just as near the opposite of the truth as he could possibly.

He would put himself at considerable inconvenience, and consider himself well paid, if he could only make an Indian miserable, and see him writhe beneath some fancied trouble. He would tease and tantalize the poor red-skins at every possible opportunity, and the good-will shown the father and his brothers was turned to hatred upon the son. One night he was caught out of his log-hut, when some half-a-dozen Indians took after him. Had it been daylight, he would have stood his ground with that number, but, in the darkness, he thought it prudent to look to his legs for safety. He had just time to gain his door ahead of his pursuers, where his sturdy wife stood ready to help him close and fasten it against them. He had frequently made the Indians run; and now, when they found the tables turned upon him, they set up a hideous yell, as they bounded against the door. They seemed to have no guns, and, after spending their fury in terrible shrieks and thumps, as they prowled round the door for an hour, they withdrew, to the great relief of the inmates of the cabin. It was a fearful hour to him, who had really never known what it was before to fear. He did not know at what moment a fire might be kindled outside his cabin, and then he knew there must be close quarters. He was on the point of trying his trusty musket upon the intruders, but his wife prevailed upon him to desist, as that would surely bring death to themselves.

John Penn, grandson of William Penn, had, very foolishly, offered a bounty for the capture or scalps of Indians, he being Lieutenant-Governor of the Colony in 1764. He was another degenerated descendant, and he did not belong to the respected Society of his grandfather.

The bounty was: "For every male above the age of ten years captured, $150; scalped, being killed, $134; for every female Indian enemy, and every male under the age of ten years captured, $130; for every female above the age of ten years scalped, being killed, $50." (!)

George La Bar, senior, liked the law, for he hated the Indians. At that time squads of men might often be seen, with George as their captain, looking for "game" which promised such reward in dollars and cents. What made this law the more heinous, was the fact that the Indians were about broken down in this part of the Colony, and a peace was concluded the very same year.

George's hostility toward the Indians was intensified by the fact that he came very near being shot by them a few years before. A scout of some thirty men went out from Hunter's settlement to rout out the Indians from Water Gap to Lehigh, near the Moravian settlement. They only found a few straggling red-skins, until, when near the Lehigh, they were suddenly surprised and scattered by five times their own force. Henry Hauser was shot down, close by the side of George. Hauser begged not to be left to be scalped by the Indians; but, as his ammunition was gone, La Bar knew that to tarry with his dying comrade would only be to court certain death, and he fled for his life. The surprise had been so sudden that the party scattered to save themselves in every direction. George fled toward the mountain, and as it was winter, and very icy, he threw off his shoes, and, on his stocking feet, soon outstripped his pursuers. Halting against the mountain-side to take breath, he looked down in the valley, and saw the Indians scalp his comrade, and then have a war-dance around the dead victim! He travelled eight miles without shoes, over the

ice and snow, before he reached the settlement.

A party returned for the body of Hauser next
day, and found it stripped naked, scalped, and
left. Hauser was from Lower Smithfield, near
Water Gap, and brother of Ulrich Hauser, an
old settler of that place.

This circumstance aroused the ire of Ulrich,
and he raised a company of thirty or forty men
in Smithfield, and they went frequently in
search of the "reds" north of the mountain.

Wherever they saw a smoke curling up
through the trees they aimed for it; and many
red scalps avenged the death of Henry.

Tom Casper, a great Indian-slayer, was with
the expedition in which Hauser was killed, as
also a little Dutchman who lived in Hunter's
settlement. He used to boast that he had killed
fourteen without getting a scratch.

CHAPTER VII.

THE SMITHFIELDS.

To fly a kite, or talk to kings;
To fill a "stick," or say wise things;
To plan a fort, tell how to fight;
To show that Liberty is Right,
    He was the man.

BENJAMIN FRANKLIN'S official life, previous to the Revolution, was spent in looking after the interests of the Colony abroad; but in 1756, the Indians had become so bloodthirsty, through the inhuman zeal of the whites, that he was sent to the front, to exercise his master-mind upon the situation.

Among his first orders, issued from Bethlehem, was the following:

"To Captain JOHN VAN ETTEN, of Upper Smithfield township, Northampton County:

"*Sir*— 1. You are to proceed immediately to raise a company of foot, consisting of thirty able men, including two sergeants, with which you are to protect the inhabitants of Upper Smithfield, assisting them while threshing out and securing their corn, and scouting from time to time as you judge necessary, on the outside of the settlement, with such of the inhabitants as may join you, to discover the enemy's approaches, and repel their attacks.

"2. For the better security of the inhabitants of that district, you are to post your men as follows: Eight at your own house, eight at Lieutenant Hyndshaw's, six with sergeant at Tishhock, and six with another sergeant at or near Henry Courtright's; and you are to settle signals, or means of sudden alarming the inhabitants, and conveying your whole strength with the militia of your district, on any necessary occasion.

"3. Every man is to be engaged for one month; and, as the Province cannot at present furnish arms or blankets to your company, you are to allow every man enlisting and bringing his own arms and blanket, a dollar for the use thereof, over and above his pay.

"4. You are to furnish your men with provisions, not exceeding the allowance mentioned in the paper herewith given to you, and your reasonable accounts for the same shall be allowed and paid.

"5. You are to keep a diary or journal of every day's transactions, and an exact account of the time when each man enters himself with you; and if any man desert or die, you are to note the time in your journal, and the time of engaging a new man in his place, and submit your journal to the inspection of the Governor when required.

"6. You are to acquaint the men that if in their ranging they meet with, or are at any time attacked by the enemy, and kill any of them, forty dollars will be allowed and paid by the Government for each scalp of an Indian enemy so killed, the same being produced, properly attested.

"7. You are to take care that your stores and provisions be not wasted.

"8. If, by any means, you gain intelligence of the designs of the enemy, or the march of any of their parties toward any part of the frontier, you are to send advice thereof to the Governor, and to the other companies in the neighborhood, as the occasion may require.

"9. You are to keep good order among your men, and prevent drunkenness and other immoralities as much as may be, and not suffer them to do any injury to the inhabitants whom they come to protect.

"10. You are to take care that the men keep their arms

clean and in good order, and that their powder always be
kept dry and fit for use.

"11. You are to make up your muster rolls at the end of
the month, in order to receive pay of your company, and to
make oath to the truth thereof before a justice of the peace,
and then transmit the same to the Governor.

"B. FRANKLIN.

"*January* 12*th*, 1756."

In writing to Governor Morgan, from Bethlehem, a day or two after, Franklin says: "I have
threatened to disband or remove the companies
already posted for the security of particular
townships, if the people would not stay on their
places, behave like men, do something for themselves, and assist the Province soldiers." He
says he found the whole settlements around
and north of Bethlehem on the very point of
giving up the whole region to the Indians. But
he soon established a line of soldiery from the
Lehigh to Bushkill, and brought order out of
chaos.

Upper Smithfield and Lower Smithfield were
township names one hundred and fifty years
ago; but the territory claimed originally by
each has changed considerably. Pike County
was cut off of Upper Smithfield, and a large part
of Monroe County was formed from Lower
Smithfield. It was the Esopus settlers who
gave the names.

Immediately after Franklin's visit to the front,
Governor Morgan visited it also; and he, at

Franklin's suggestion, established a line of forts, or block-houses, reaching from the Susquehanna, at Shamokin, to Fort Hamilton, (Stroudsburg,) and up the Delaware to Walpack Bend or Bushkill. A line also followed the Blue Ridge, and reached to the Lehigh. The forts were anything but what we would now call forts, being merely stakes driven into the ground and then banked up with earth, with a sort of log-hut in each corner, in the inside, for barracks, and to accommodate the settlers' families, as, from time to time, they were driven in for safety. The one generally supposed to have been near the mouth of the Bushkill was called Fort Hyndshaw, after the Lieutenant appointed by Franklin. The argument in favor of locating this fort near the mouth of the Bushkill is taken from a report which mentions its being near a large creek; but I think the reporter meant near a large creek which comes into the river on the opposite side. I base my conclusions on the fact that the road from Fort Hamilton to Fort Hyndshaw led past Depui's, which was along the river, and that we are told it was an "open road from Depui's to Fort Hyndshaw." Now, by following up the river flats, it would not be an open road to Bushkill, for there is, even now, an impassable barrier on this side of the river. The fort was on the flats, *opposite* Flat Brook.

Depui's house was stone, and that was stock-
aded, and a swivel gun was mounted at each
corner. This was sometimes called Depui's
fort, and was, in reality, more of a fort than any
of the others.

Depui was never in fear of the surrounding
Indians; at least, not until after 1737, for he
had lived among them in perfect security, as
had his father before him. But when the French
began to exert their wicked influence upon them,
reaching down from Canada, then Depui became alarmed, and he and his neighbors begged
earnestly for colonial help. Such calls were
always respected, and help came. When Depui
asked for soldiers, he always informed the Governor that he had plenty of provision to sup-
port them.

In all the public life of the original Depuis,
reported by various officials of the Colony who
called upon them, I find only one charge, and
that is by James Young, "Commissary-General
of ye Musters."

On a tour of inspection in 1756, he reached
Depui's, June 24th, and says:

"At 7 P. M. came to Samuel Depui's. Mus-
tered that part of Captain Wetherhold's company that are stationed here, a lieutenant and
twenty-six men, all regularly enlisted for six
months, as are the rest of his company. Round
Depui's house is a large but slight stockade,

with a swivel gun mounted on each corner.
Mr. Depui was not at home, his son, with a son
of Mr. Brodhead, keeping house. They ex-
pressed themselves as if they thought the Province was obliged to them for allowing this party
to be in their house; also made use of very ar-
rogant expressions of the commissioners, and
the people of Philadelphia in general. They
make a mere merchandise of the people stationed here.

"Provincial stores: thirteen good muskets,
three cartridge-boxes, thirteen pounds powder,
twenty-two pounds lead."

The most of the men furnished their own
arms and blankets, and thus received seven
instead of six dollars per month.

The first Depui we have any account of was
Nicholas, who was an old man in 1737; and
in 1756, we read of Nicholas, Aaron, and Samuel
as prominent. These were, perhaps, the sons
of the first Nicholas. In the Revolution, the
most prominent was still Nicholas, who was then
esquire, and who may have been a son or grandson of the first. It was always a prominent
family, and well to do. They had a grist-mill
as early as 1755, and we know a stone church
was built at Shawnee in 1752, which was torn
down but a few years ago, and replaced by
brick. The old corner-stone still graces the

new church. It was built originally as Dutch and Presbyterian.

Daniel Brodhead's place was the only clearing between Depui's and Fort Hamilton, and here soldiers were stationed in 1755. Stroud took hold of the land between Brodhead's and La Bar's. In 1757, Captain Van Etten had charge of the forts Hyndshaw and Hamilton, with men at Depui's. April 25th, he sent Sergeant Leonard Denn to Depui's for subsistence, with two men. Having reached about two miles from Depui's, they were fired upon by a party of Indians, and the sergeant was killed. The two men returned to the fort, gave the alarm, the body was found, naked and scalped, and carried to Depui's and buried.

Two or three days previous to this, a young man by name of Countryman was killed and scalped within three hundred yards of Fort Hamilton.

On the 23d of June, five men were attacked near Brodhead's house, and one John Tidd was killed. A squad was sent out of the fort, and when near Brodhead's, upwards of thirty Indians were discovered, who, seeing the soldiers, endeavored to get between them and the weakened fort. The captain dropped one Indian, and then they made off. On the same day, a scout of thirteen men arrived at the fort, searching for the wife of Edward Marshall, who had been shot some time before. The firing had attracted them to the spot. The next day the Jersey party accompanied the captain to the scene of the fight, and found the body of the dead man, and also the dead carcasses of fifteen cattle, horses, and hogs. The Indians had driven away two beeves, with other plunder carried off.

The house of Peter La Bar was within Fort Hamilton, and his was the only clearing near the fort for a long time. Wherever there was a clearing at this time, soldiers were detailed to keep guard while the men got in their harvest. From 1752 to 1759 the war front was from Bethlehem to Depui's and Fort Hyndshaw, and the settlers along this front had a rough time of it. Many gave up in despair, and left their improvements; their log-houses were burnt, and their harvests left unreaped. During this time, petition after petition, numerously signed, was sent in to the Colonial Government for help. Those below the mountain asked, again and again, that the Blue Ridge should be the line of defence, and that all beyond should be left to the Indians. Such petition was never granted. In 1758, James Burd made an examination of the outposts in Northampton County, going up as far as Fort Hyndshaw. He said that south of the mountain was a fine country, but that north of the mountain it was an entire barren wilderness, not capable of improvement. What would he think of it now?

Of Depui's, he says, "This is a fine plantation, situate upon the river Delaware, one hundred miles from Philadelphia, and thirty-five from Easton. They go in boats from here to Philadelphia, which carry about twenty-two tons. There is a pretty good stockade here, with four swivels mounted, and good accommodations for soldiers."

He further says: "Reviewed this garrison, and found twenty-two good men, fifty pounds powder, one hundred and twenty-five pounds lead, no flints, a great quantity of beef, I suppose eight months' provisions for a company, but no flour. Plenty of flour at the mill, about three hundred yards from the fort. The country apply for a company to be stationed here. Extremely cold." This was March 3d. There was no opening through the Water Gap, and Wind Gap was the communicating road with the south side of the mountain.

The Indians stood out stoutly and long to hold their hunting-ground along the Delaware above the Water Gap. But they were forced, at length, to give up all hope, and the place that knew them knows them no more. They gave up the contest in 1764.

About a mile above the Water Gap, on a

high bank of the river, is an old Indian burial-ground. It is overgrown with large trees, but some of the mounds are still visible. The Delaware Water Gap was a favorite home of the Indians, and the stone relics of the race have been picked up in great numbers throughout this vicinity. Their bark canoes here floated on the lake-like waters of the Delaware, as on a charmed element, suspending the joyous inmates of the tiny craft as if in mid-air between the towering mountains of the Kittatinny.

But the canoe is no more, and the natives have disappeared. Only the curiously wrought arrow-heads, their tomahawks and stone pestles, remain to show that they had ever been inhabitants here.

George's father used to relate to his boy various scenes of blood and slaughter enacted by the savages in his own neighborhood, the most terrible of which was perpetrated in 1755, during the descent upon the whites of some two hundred Indians under that apostate Moravian, Teedyuscung. Edward Marshall, who accomplished the great Indian Walk, by which the Indians were cheated out of a vast hunting-ground, lived, at this time, at or near the present village of Slateford. Though Marshall was not to blame for the Walk, for he did it as a hired man, though he never received the five hun-

4

dred acres of land promised him, still the Indians remembered the part he had taken upon
himself, and they determined to retaliate. They
fired on a company attending a funeral, on the
road just below his house, killing none, but
driving most of the settlers across the river.
The burying-ground was on a high bluff, just
back of the lime-kilns at Portland. That old
grave-yard is still to be seen there, with old
headstones of common sandstone and slate,
with dates reaching back to 1764. Not to be
foiled, the Indians, or a party of them, surrounded the house of Marshall, who was not
at home. They shot his daughter as she was
trying to escape, the ball entering her right
shoulder and coming out below the left breast:
yet she got away from them, and recovered.
They took Marshall's wife, who was not in
condition to make a rapid flight, some miles
with them, and killed her. They had attacked
Marshall's house in 1748, and then killed one
of his sons. Though thirsting for Marshall's
blood through many years, yet they seem to
have always feared him, and usually undertook
their bloody work when he was from home.
They never gained their object, for, though he
had many hairbreadth escapes, he finally died
a natural death, after attaining an old age.
These occurrences took place only a few years
before the birth of George, but were told him

when yet fresh in the memory of his father and of his neighbors.

During the boyhood of George the only mill for grinding was across the mountain, and thither all the grain was carried, on horseback, for the Mount Bethel region. Those from the more southern part of the settlement went to Easton for the same purpose. The corn was generally pounded in mortars, as was the custom with the Indians. As the mill was so inconvenient, George's father frequently set him to pounding up the wheat also. The large mortar his father had made, but the pestle was obtained of the Indians. It was a dressed stone, about two feet long, and about three inches in diameter. For bolting the wheat he made two rough sieves, one finer than the other, and the flour came out a kind of Graham, which made good healthy bread.

There was no road through the Water Gap at this time, and many were the trips made by George, on horseback, over the mountain, by way of Tat's Gap, to Stroudsburg, to mill. He always waited until his bag of wheat was ground, and then made his way back. It took the whole day to make the round trip, and, unless the clever miller asked him to dine with him, George was a hungry boy when he returned home. There was no store nearer than Easton. One mile north of Martin's Creek — named

after Colonel Martin of the Revolution — was
the ancient Bethel Church, (from which came
Mount Bethel,) of which the zealous David
Brainerd was the founder. At this place he
built a rude cabin-parsonage, and made it his
headquarters while laboring, far and near, for
the spiritual welfare of both whites and Indians.
At the time of which we write, a meeting-
house, built of logs, had just been set up at
Williamsburg. It has long since passed away,
with the congregation. On a recent visit to
its old grave-yard, I found a stone noting a
death in 1750.

A ferry was started at a very early day, by
one Dill, and called for a long time Dill's
Ferry. This place has since been called
Decker's Ferry, Mount Bethel, and Portland. We are waiting now for it to be named
again. The place seems to have suffered for a
name ever since the first true name of Dill's
Ferry was discarded. It was at this place that
the people of Mount Bethel met to rejoice, with
those on the opposite side of the river, over the
victory of the American arms in the Revolution. At this time there was quite a settlement
on the Jersey side of the river — the timid ones,
who had come up to the front in earlier days,
and then, for more personal security, placed
the river in front. But the Pennsylvania settlement was always preferable, on account of a

better soil. The wooded region south of the Blue Ridge, on the Jersey side of the river, was George's early favorite hunting-ground, and many a deer and bear he has there brought down, and carried on his back to his home on the other side of the river.

CHAPTER VIII.

RUSTIC LIFE.

Inured to sternest life of toil,
Which to no danger showed recoil,
The sire transmitted to the son
The hardy nature he had won.

INHERITING the strong characteristics of his stern ancestors, whose lives of toil, privation, and self-reliance had helped them to surmount every difficulty that a frontier, wilderness life of trial and danger could possibly throw across their way, young George grew up a robust lad, skillful with his gun, or with oxen and wooden plow. The rude shanty, first planted by his grandfather, had been replaced by a house comparatively modern, and contentment bloomed upon a home quite as happy as the most refined of to-day. The schoolmaster had not entered this part of Pennsylvania, and a thousand indispensable blessings

of the nineteenth century were then unknown,
and consequently not longed for. The labor
of the field was his employment, and his gun
and fishing-rod his amusements, which were
turned to good account in furnishing supplies
for the table of wooden plates and spoons.
Health glowed upon his countenance and
cheerfulness from his heart. His wants were
few, and on himself he depended to gain them.
By the blazing fire, in the long winter nights,
his father would interest his boy with accounts
of perils and dangers among his red neighbors.
To him was pointed out the place, but a mile
distant, where a family was butchered for some
trivial offence by the mad savages. The family muskets were kept loaded and primed for
many long years, ready for any emergency that
might arise.

Others of the persecuted from beyond the
broad Atlantic kept coming in, from year to
year, until "Hunter's settlement" became, comparatively, quite a populous region, and the
Indians began to suspect that their safety lay
north of the Kittatinny Mountain. The original name of Hunter's settlement was finally
replaced by Mount Bethel, which name it has
retained ever since. This settlement was
planted very early at three points, near Martin's Creek, at Richmond, and at Williamsburg,
probably about 1730.

When those places were first settled, it was only the most daring who ventured to strike boldly out and plant themselves in the very midst of their wild neighbors. This the La Bar family had done at the very first move of the French immigrants.

As George was now growing up to manhood, he found many leaving their village block-houses to settle around his father's plantation, to clear the land and till the soil. Peace, plenty, and comfort beget happiness and contentment, and the wilderness became, very soon, comparatively joyous and glad.

The Indians had fallen gradually back; the terrible fires which had previously swept from the mountains to the river, killing or stunting the trees and presenting a vast barren, blackened picture, that had been repictured every year, were becoming less frequent, and the wooded scene was putting on new beauty and freshness. The mountains at that time were barren and naked, and the patches of large trees which we now find on the low grounds in Mount Bethel, have all grown up within the one hundred and ten or one hundred and twenty-five years since the Indians ceased to burn the woods to rout out their game.

But society thickened around, and that social intercourse, which adds so much to human happiness, brought forward that "good time" when their happiness was all that could be desired. George thought he was living in a favored day, enjoying blessings which his grandfather knew nothing of when he first came to this country. In fact he could hardly see then what could be added to his privileges. He has seen an improvement since.

"Where ignorance is bliss, 't is folly to be wise."

The La Bar family had multiplied already so that there were several Johns and four or five Georges. The father George was called "little George;" our George was "curly George;" there was a "big George" and a "faithful George," all living in close proximity.

Old Samuel Pipher moved into the neighborhood about eighty years ago. He was a very pleasant Dutchman, and the young folks of the neighborhood used to gather at his house frequently to have a good time. At that time there was a good deal of open-air exercise in the field and of open-air sport wherever and whenever young people could get together.

John Staples came to this country from England, on that tea-vessel which created such a stir around Boston Harbor in 1773. He had an interest in the cargo, until he saw it dumped into the water, when he became more interested in the people who had become so exasperated by the oppressive acts of his Government as to inflict a great loss upon individuals. He came to Pennsylvania and joined the American army as a private. He fought through the war, and was then offered the office of colonel, which he declined, on the ground that the position had not been offered before.

After the war, Staples settled above the mountain, near Bossard's, raised a very large family, lived to a ripe old age, and when he died his descendants numbered hundreds. To-day, the Staples family number thousands.

Joseph Drake was prominent in the Revolution, and his father, John, was an early settler north of the Blue Ridge. The Drake family are numerous now in Monroe County.

John Fenner was a Revolutionary patriot, from Mount Bethel. His father lived just above Easton, on the Jersey side, having settled there at an early day, and there he died. Nearly all the descendants pushed up into what is now Monroe County, and this stock does its share in forming the population of the county.

David Bush was also an early settler above the mountain, and, despite the general clearing up of the country, the Bushes flourish luxuriantly.

Antoine Dutot, a Frenchman, was driven from Hayti, during the insurrection there, in

1794. He was a man of property, having owned a large plantation, but he was glad to escape with his life. He got separated from his wife, and landed at Philadelphia without her. Being a Frenchman, and acquainted with Stephen Girard when he was a resident also of Hayti, he assisted Dutot, and induced him to go up the river and settle in Pennsylvania. He finally located himself at Delaware Water Gap, purchasing here a large tract of land, which he laid out for an extensive inland city. But, alas for the great city! its founder was too superficial, and built such temporary houses that not one of them is standing to-day. Dutotsburg had to be rebuilt, and the city is not. Dutot built roads and streets where roads and streets were not wanted by anybody but himself; and, though a busy, enterprising man, his judgment and his labor proved but failures.

Antoine was a gay old Frenchman, with a romantic taste, while his ruffled shirt, his silk stockings, and his silver knee-buckles, with his broadcloth, were faultless; but his slaves were not the slaves he had in Hayti, nor was the product of this soil at all tropical. The out-go was sure, but the income was treacherous.

Dutot supposed his wife had been slaughtered in the great massacre on the island, and when he came to Water Gap, he looked upon himself as a widower. He had been here over two years, and had already made considerable progress in the way of making a choice for another helpmeet. The past dark, dangerous, and mysterious scenes through which he had passed, had become somewhat hidden by the new light of promise that shed its joy around him. Even the great wealth he had been forced to quit so hurriedly, to be appropriated by the French negroes, and the gold he had buried in the hope of returning to that island again—all this was gradually losing its hold upon his mind. It don't take a Frenchman long to forget the past, when the future is lit up with promise. The day was fixed when he was to have a wife to call his own again, and there were no French negroes here to kill another wife. He was safe now, and would be henceforth. Only one day more, and the desired knot shall be tied! Just in time! The original Mrs. Dutot was not killed! She has found her husband, and the marriage is indefinitely postponed.

Among the names of early settlers, not already mentioned, in Mount Bethel, are those of Mann, Beck, Miller, Allen, Kennedy, Musselman, Kuntz, Frey, Detrich, Meyers, Schneider, Frederick, etc.

CHAPTER IX.

THE REVOLUTION.

A dark cloud rises from the East,
  The red men claim the West,
A patriot few, than all the least,
  Resolved to make the test;
Resolved, in God, to strike to be
A nation separate and free!

Though some a timid faith might show,
  And linger in the rear,
A larger number asked to show
  What might be founded here,
Assured the Right must win, succeed,
When patriots dared to fight and bleed!

AND now lowered the war-clouds of the Revolution, and with these came trouble, commotion, and trial. Not that these settlers did not love their chosen country sufficiently to go forth to defend their country's honor; but that this going forth left their homes, especially in this county, too often exposed and unprotected from the arm of their red-skinned neighbors, while it took, also, the laborer from the field and cut off the supply of game from the woods. George was now twelve years of age, and he well remembers the opening days of that bold and daring undertaking which would presume to measure arms with Great Britain.

No people but the hardy pioneers of America and their sons would, for a moment, have harbored such a wild and hazardous purpose. But the strong physical man exhibited the same strong will and mind that nobly dared to do or die. Oh, what terrible surgings between hope and despair, again and again, lifted up or sank the American heart! How deeply was every family interested in the doubtful contest! A small people, without means, without prestige in any other war except that which necessity forced upon them in defending themselves against a race of natives who were exasperated by the wrong dealing of the white leaders — without anything except right and a strong will. David attacking the giant, and the pigmy prevails!

George was too young to philosophize upon the probable result of an armed resistance to British authority; and, as he heard the thundering of the cannon in the distance, he would have liked nothing better than to have been in the front with his father's musket. Boy as he was, he knew how to level his gun to tell upon his mark. But they said he was too young. His father looked upon the rebellion as premature and unwise. He thought the colonies too weak, as yet, to resist the arm of the mother country, and that the mad undertaking would but result in a heavier oppression and tyranny.

He had had a broken leg, and to this he looked for an excuse to keep him out of the American army. Not that he was opposed to the Yankee cause, but because he considered it hopeless, he would have nothing to do with it, if he could have his own way.

The "game leg" did not seem to interfere with the busy inclination of its possessor, for his locomotive powers seemed to be unimpaired. He could chase a deer or an Indian with wonderful agility. This fact led the new authorities to suspect there was too much "game" in the leg. Accordingly, it was resolved to try him, as the following incident will show:

One day, George was with his father, not far from the house, splitting rails. A stranger, in citizen's dress, came to him, and told him he was a spy from the British army, and asked to stay with him all night. His father said he never turned anybody off who wanted a night's lodging. It was near night, and they went to the house. Soon after entering, the pretended British spy, looking out a crack of the door, said the Yankees were after him, and asked where he should go. The father said he could go up stairs. George's mother said, "No! get out door, and be off." A moment more, and a half-a-dozen Yankee soldiers, in uniform, came in; the spy had played his game, and La Bar was pronounced a Tory. He was at once arrested, leg and all, and taken, that night, to Easton.

George's mother was greatly troubled that night, and he, to comfort her, told her he would follow him in the morning, and offer himself to take his father's place. But she knew his generous offer would not be accepted, nor would such a substitute afford her the desired relief.

Early the next morning, Mrs. La Bar set out, on horseback, for Easton, whither she supposed her husband had been taken. Arriving there, she found he had been bailed by Squire Levis and Abraham La Bar, a cousin, who soon after was a colonel in the Revolutionary army. She succeeded in proving the leg unfit for military duty, and the man was permitted to take it home again, to the joy of the woman and the satisfaction of the children, who had been left alone at home.

A short time after this, his horses were seized by an officer, and taken to Squire Depui's, at Shawnee. He got his horses by swearing allegiance to the Government of the United States. Another horse was captured by one John Herring, who seems to have assumed his own authority for so doing. This horse was never returned, and never paid for. Free speech and a high-tempered disposition, with an inclination to retaliate, had the same effect now upon those who were heart and soul in sympathy with the rebel cause, to create enemies, just as the Indians were made so before. The senior George La Bar was called a Tory for these reasons.

Fire-arms were scarce in the Revolution, and a requisition was made, early in the war, for all such arms to be brought forward for the emergency. La Bar could spare one or two old shot-guns, but his own tried musket he kept for a long time, hid in a hollow tree in the woods. Was he to blame for this, when much of his meat had to be brought out of the woods?

Northampton County had so long been the battle-ground in the Indian troubles, that the settlers were heartily sick of blood and carnage; and when the Revolution opened, very many in the county resisted the measure to the utmost. It was with the greatest difficulty that they could be brought up to take the oath of allegiance to the new Government. Many "skedadled" to Jersey rather than submit to what they considered a rebellion that would soon be crushed. A few joined the Indians, and Tories were skulking everywhere, to keep out of reach of the authorities.

Some were arrested, and carried to Easton. The citizens begged that such prisoners might be taken to Philadelphia, or to Reading, as they feared a descent might be made upon that town by the sympathizing multitude of Tories.

In none of the confederated colonies, perhaps, were the Revolutionary patriots placed in such trying circumstances as those of Northampton County. They had enemies in front and rear, and none but the truest could stand such a test.

July 1st, 1776, the whole land force of Pennsylvania consisted of one thousand four hundred and thirty-two men. The British lion in front, Indians and Tories in the rear! surely there was ground for doubts. To us, at this time, there would seem to be no hope, no ray of promise. It was like cutting loose from a stanch ship in mid-ocean, when fog and darkness were thick and foreboding, to trust in a tiny lifeboat with only an oar!

But the tiny little lifeboat was cared for by an overruling Providence, and safely, gloriously guided into the desired haven of peace and security. The new flag was planted triumphantly on a free soil, and a glowing future awaited the new Republic. The first step in the grand experiment had proved a success fully up to the hope of the most sanguine. The corner-stone was well laid, and the great Temple of Liberty began, at once, to go up toward a grand and symmetrical building.

5

The sacrifice had been great, but the promise of the future amply satisfied all. A new country of free people, away from the contaminating influence of kings and emperors — a people governing and being governed by themselves, without any grade except the grade of honest worth and manly purpose, where the highest point of honor was open to the humblest subject. The like had not been known in modern times, and the world looked on with wonder and astonishment: the common world rejoiced and took courage.

CHAPTER X.

AFTER THE WAR.

> At length, despite the long delay,
> The smoke of battle cleared away,
> To cheer with a more perfect day;
> And patriot hearts now joyed indeed :
> The war was o'er, their country freed,
> And not in vain did any bleed.

YES, the Revolution was over, and there was general rejoicing. Even the doubters were glad, although they had tried not to help to such an issue. They did not like the name of Tory, and denied its application to them, because they were not at heart against their country, nor especially in favor of British

power, but they considered the movement unwise and without hope. They were glad that
the British had been defeated, but their rejoicing was a quiet joy, for the shame that they
had taken no hearty part in the great work put
a muzzle upon their mouths as a very natural
consequence.

Meetings of rejoicing were held all over the
confederated colonies, and there was such a
meeting at Dill's Ferry, and George was there.
If he could not battle for victory, he could rejoice with those who had fought and won. "It
was a high old time."

George was called the son of a Tory, and a
rough neighbor seeing him, and being excited
with a combination of joy and of anger, drew
up his gun, pointed it at the young man, and
said, "Get away, you young Tory, or I will
shoot you down." More sober-minded men
interfered, and the fatal shot was not fired.
There may have been too much whisky, but
the joy was sincere, for it penetrated to the
very marrow of the inside man. The day had
been so long and so dark, the struggle had
been so desperate and painful, the victory so
barely won, that, altogether, it made a most
hearty joy and thanksgiving.

But the war was over, and the people were
poor, the country poorer than before the war,
many lives had been lost, a paper money

almost worthless, many crippled and maimed for life, many widows and orphans — yet, to cover all this was *Liberty*, and the rejoicing was for this. The very name of Liberty had a signification it never had before. There beamed from the fair name a halo of light and love and blessedness that could be felt and seen. Well might there be unbounded joy over a noble aim so nobly achieved.

Thankful should we be to-day that the fruit of their labor yet continues to grow, to bless their descendants, though almost a century has elapsed since they went forth to battle for the right. May centuries yet to come show the same holy trust faithfully preserved, to be handed down, on and on, to the latest generation of time!

George senior, after accumulating a good property in Mount Bethel, and after rearing a large family, took it in his head to go West in his old age. About the year 1808 he sold out the most of his property to his son Isaac, loaded up his wagon, and set out for the long drive to Ohio. He was then about eighty-five years old. He had a good team of horses, and his wagon was arranged to be his hotel on the road. He took his wife with him, but left all his children behind. As he had more than one load of goods to take along, he hired George junior to take his team and wagon, and go with him. It was no small matter to move to Ohio then. It was a long, tedious drive, over very bad roads, with very few bridges. But it had been done, and he would do it. His friends tried hard to talk him out of such an expedition in his old days; but his strong self-will prevailed, and they started. Crossing the mountains through Tat's Gap, the old man turned to look upon his old homestead for the last time; but no feeling of regret touched his hard old heart, for, instead of a blessing, he pronounced almost a curse upon it as his eyes turned from it forever.

It took two weeks, through an almost unbroken wilderness, to reach the point aimed for — two long, tedious weeks of shaking and jolting, with the camping by the way. But the stern old man reached Ohio, and was satisfied. George remained a few days, and, after another two weeks' drive, reached his home again.

The old man lost his wife when he was ninety-eight, and, when one hundred, he married again. At one hundred and five he died, a poor man; but he died where he wished to die, and was buried in the soil of Ohio.

CHAPTER XI.

A VISIT TO THE CENTENARIAN.

"A relic-hunting I would go."

IN the summer of 1869, having a desire to
shake hands and to exchange thoughts
with one whose history reaches back past a
century, I set out, early one morning, to grat-
ify this wish. Taking a train at the Water
Gap, I soon arrived at Spragueville, the nearest railroad station to the point I had in view.
Obtaining the proper directions, I found I had
a three-mile walk before me, through a broken,
wooded region, the principal product of which
was railroad ties, cord-wood, bark, hoop-poles,
and rocks. The rocks are what is termed in
real estate "fast property," and they are really
abundant, so much so, that I found they were
permitted to lay about fast and loose, regard-
less of the danger of being appropriated by
trespassers, who do "hook on" to some of the
other products of the country.

But I had begun my three-mile travel toward my destination over a "back road," which
in Pennsylvania English means a road that
supervisors never expect to work down below
the smoothness of a magnified grater. This

road was made for oxen, mules, and pedestrians like myself, and I pressed on, too much concerned about my *footing* to become especially poetical by the music of the birds singing around me, or by the wildness of the scenery which touched so pointedly the toe of my boot, to the sudden shaking of the corporeal and the mental. Between these jars I did manage to wonder why Nature had not scattered some of this surplus *hardness* out on prairie-land, for the building of cellar-walls and the like.

Those three miles were long, but I got over them, having passed but one human habitation, and I now discovered a "clearing" which looked quite farmlike; at least, it so looked in the distance. Just before me, and close by the woods from which I had emerged, surrounding a small one-story house, I saw what reminded me of "Oysters in Every Style." There were stone out-buildings, stone fences, stone stacks around stumps, stone paths, stones round and flat, stones in rows, and stones lying around promiscuously.

In that little house, with such a *hard* surrounding, lives Mr. George La Bar, who is now in his *one hundred and seventh year!* Though I wondered at the profusion with which Nature had here strewn the earth with rocks and stones, I wondered more at his choice, who, nearly fifty years ago, had chosen such a spot to labor and toil upon, in order to build a home for himself and family. After I had heard his story of ups and downs in life, I suspected he had tired of his kind, who had dealt roughly with him, and he then sought out a place in the wilderness, with the least possible temptation for any to settle near enough to crowd him again.

I had been cautioned by some of the old man's relations against being too fast in my efforts for a good, long, free talk. So, when I knocked at the door, I thought I knew just how to do it. I entered, where I had never been before, introduced myself as best I could, and began talking with the aged daughter, who, with two or three of *her* grandchildren, lives with the old father. Some of these great-great-grandchildren are adults. The old man has never been dependent upon his children or his children's children, and is not now, for he keeps his own house and his own table! Since the time when man's term of life was shortened to threescore and ten, was the like ever known? Never in the history of man!

Mr. La Bar sat before the embers smouldering in an open, old-fashioned fire-place, and took but little notice of me, having merely raised his head when I came into the house. In order to approach the old gentleman as gently as possible, I had been directing my conversation for some moments toward the old-lady daughter, and, after waiting in vain to have him address a word to me, I turned to him and said, "Well, Mr. La Bar, how do you do?" Quick as thought he answered by saying, "I am doing well enough." This was a settler which knocked all my cautious arrangements into pi! But, not to give up the field, I backed up and tried it again with another question, when he began to ask in return, and the ice—or stone—was broken, and I drew him into a sociable conversation. This had been much more interesting had he been more familiar with dates. He has lived all these years without any education except experience. As is usual with such persons, his memory is his store-house record, and it is full of reminiscences of the past, though not always reliable in regard to dates.

He is a hale and hearty old man even yet, and looks more like a man of sixty-five or seventy than one who has numbered his five score and six years. That flabbiness of skin and muscle which is peculiar to most aged persons is an exception in his case. His cheeks are as smooth as my own of forty years, and the backs of his hands exhibit the same unusual feature. He is a man of medium height — he stoops slightly now, but I think he has always been round-shouldered — a full chest, broad shoulders, and tapers down to small feet and ankles and small hands. His head is well supplied with not the whitest hair, though his beard is white. The head is not large, with blue eyes, heavy eyebrows, cheek-bones somewhat prominent, moderately high forehead, a nose slightly hooked, and, on the whole, a fair old face to look upon.

He has always been a man of toil, always a farmer, a great hunter, as long as there was any game to be found in the mountains, often lying in the woods, wherever night might overtake him — he has thus slept in the woods since he was a hundred years old! — been sick only three times in his life, once with yellow fever, the camp fever, and once typhoid — always a good eater, denying himself nothing, at any time, which his appetite craved. He has almost a voracious appetite for food now, always chewed tobacco, has smoked long, and smokes very frequently now.

He has never been drunk, never intemperate, but, living through the time when the bottle stood on every family cupboard, he never showed himself "odd" in refusing to take an occasional glass. He never could be prevailed upon to drink when he was not thirsty, and he would not permit alcohol to exercise dominion over him. He says he always considered a man a fool who could be overcome by whisky. Temperance in eating and drinking was always his motto and his guide, though he confesses to intemperance in overwork and exposure. But temperance in the former enabled his physical system to bear up under the latter.

Every day he takes exercise, even yet, with his axe, felling the trees in the woods for his old-times fireplace, and occasionally gets out railroad ties. During the summer of 1869 he felled trees and peeled, with his own hands, three wagon-loads of bark, which one of his youngest boys, a lad of sixty years, hauled to market for the old chopper! Not two years ago he was out hunting bees in the woods.

After talking an hour or so, I went over to see one of his sons, who lives "on the farm," and when I returned I found the old man missing. Inquiring for him, I was told he had "gone to the woods to chop!" That was just what I wanted to see; so, taking the youngest great-great-grandson with me, I went over to the woods, some three-quarters of a mile distant, where I tried to take observations from a distance; but his brood of dogs soon gave the alarm. I was observed, and came up at once. He excused himself for coming to the woods by saying he thought I had gone home. But I saw him chop, a thing I never expect to see another man do who has on his head one hundred and six years, and now well on another year!

Taking the old man by the hand to bid him good-by, I remarked that I had enjoyed my visit very much, when he surprised me by saying he would come down during the summer, and show me how to catch rock-fish from the Delaware. I took him, at once, at his word, and told him I would come up after him in a few weeks, to which he agreed. After hearing several fish-stories, while he stood leaning on the handle of his axe, I left him, he returning to his home, and I wending my way back toward the depot.

It was really wonderful to see a man of so many years wielding an axe. There seems to be no give up to him, and he is determined to be no idler, so long as he lives and is able to have it otherwise. In walking he uses merely a small stick, and this he always leaves outside the door when he enters the house. He has a more finished cane which he carries when he goes from home. He says he looks upon himself as one who has lived far beyond the usual bounds of human life, and he feels like one alone in the world, for all his old associates have passed away long since, many of them three generations ago. He is ready and waiting, but must work while he waits.

CHAPTER XII.

BROTHER AND SISTER.

We took a ride, one day,
And then a walk;
I held the reins and led the way,
'T was his to talk.

A FEW weeks later I ran up to see the old man and make arrangements to have him come down and "show me how to catch rock-fish." Arriving at his house, I was disappointed to find him away from home, he having gone on business to Stroudsburg. The old-lady daughter informed me that he had talked of his engagement, and that he would come with me at any time I might call for him. She said I must come with a horse and carriage, as he would not ride on the cars. So I set a day and returned home.

At the appointed time I was at the old man's door again. Eight miles, and the latter part of the journey required careful driving. He was out enjoying the open air. The daughter soon had him "fixed up," and we were facing toward the Water Gap. It was a beautiful September day, and the old man enjoyed the ride finely. I think he must have known that I did not chew tobacco, for the first man we met he hailed for a chew. I had some cigars in my pocket, and these we appropriated to add variety to the already odd picture within the carriage. Arriving at the "Half-way House," the horse was thirsty. The old man said he was "dry" too. So I inquired for the "best," and he took "some." Now I don't believe in the merits of whisky, but here was a man who had lived when everybody believed there *was* merit in whisky, and I did believe it would not hurt him. I noticed, too, that he took a very small "smaller," and he said he always had drank only the *smallers*. He always had a mind strong enough to keep right-minded, and his great age proves that whisky had not robbed him of any of his days. Alas, how many have been robbed by it!

But the horse was no longer thirsty, and the carriage inmates were no longer "dry," so, after lighting the inevitable cigar, we rolled onward. I never felt so honored in my life. Everybody and all his relations, on our way, greeted us with special notice and attention. We were "the observed of all observers." It may be a country fashion, but I took it differently. Old Grandfather La Bar does not *ride* out often—he *walks* and *works;* but everybody, far and near, has heard of the old centenarian, and all were anxious to see him. No one, in his right mind, can help respecting and even honoring extreme old age. This is very right, and it did me good to see it manifested, without an exception, by every one we passed.

We reached our destination at a late dining-hour, and after showing my guest around, we sat down on the piazza to chat and smoke. Being called away from him a few moments, when I returned I found he was among the missing. Inquiring—for I had pledged myself for his well-being and safe return—I learned he was seen "making tracks" toward the Gap; so I hurried on and soon overtook him, plodding hurriedly along about half a mile down the Gap road. He seemed much surprised to be overhauled so soon by me. I asked him why he had left me so hastily, and told him I expected him to remain all night with me. He said he thought he had plenty of time to walk down to his sister's, and as he had heard she was sick, he would go there, and stop with me when he returned. I told him he had better go back with me, and I would take him down in a carriage the next day. But he refused, and, as I was determined to be faithful to my trust, I walked with him. The sister he spoke of is the youngest of the family, a girl of eighty-six, who lives five miles from the Water Gap, near the place where he was born. So on we walked and talked, and I thought no more of rock-fish for the present.

In about an hour we arrived at Slateford, three and a half miles. Here are some half-a-dozen old acquaintances, whose ages range from seventy-five to eighty-five years. We called upon old Mr. and Mrs. Hallet, Mr. and Mrs. Pipher, who could scarcely believe their own eyes. Oh, it did my heart good to see these old people meet! Every word, every gesture, seemed to be so frank, so friendly and open-hearted. Tears of joy there were, and a shaking of hands that reached to the bottom of the soul; and many honest words of truth and soberness, and life and death, were spoken. Very soon the whole village was gathered together, and joy and gladness sparkled in every eye, while a true spirit of human kindness, good feeling, and fellowship could be read in every countenance more distinctly than by words. I was more than paid for my dusty walk, and felt even more honored than I had been in the earlier part of the day, while riding with my old friend in another county.

While men are yet in middle life, and full of its business and anxieties, whatever be their social intercourse, we suspect that their whole heart and feeling are not in their expressions of kindly greeting; but when we see the aged grasp each other by the hand, those who have outlived the more anxious duties of life, we know they mean just what they say.

We walked on, reaching the sister's about sunset, and there was joy again. *She was not sick—she was working in the garden!* I left the old brother and young sister, promising to come again at an early day, walked a short distance to the station, took the cars, and returned.

CHAPTER XIII.

OLD STORIES.

Not many lives run smooth throughout,
    Unknown to loss or care,
But heaviest burdens make those stout
    Who have the most to bear.

AFTER a few days I went after my old friend with horse and carriage, and found him satisfied with his visit at his sister's, and ready to face toward home. We came past the old homestead of his earlier married life. Though he first lived a few years in the house with his father-in-law, yet here the most of his children were born, and some of them grew up. There, he said, he should have been satisfied; there he should have remained. It was a snug farm near Slateford. The land was smooth, and produced well, but his boys thought the farm too small, and longed for more room,

6

more land. He finally sold out, for four thousand five hundred dollars, with a view of going West, whither his old father had gone, but, governed again by others, he did not go, and, finally, bought a large tract of land, with a mill upon it, in what is now Monroe County. It was called the Long property, and situated on the Analomink. At this time wheat was three dollars per bushel, and he thought milling would pay largely; but a depression in real estate followed, with a corresponding fall in grain. He had applied his four thousand five hundred dollars toward paying for the property, which left a debt of less than a thousand dollars. In spite of careful living and hard work, the debt kept accumulating until, after a struggle of eleven years, he was forced to sell, when he found himself with only three hundred dollars ahead. He rented for two years, and then bought two hundred and nine acres of "back-wood land" for three hundred and nine dollars. On that is his home to-day. Like his grandfather, he now began right in the woods to clear a place to raise his bread and to plant a home. But the grandsire was a young man, he an old man with grandchildren. Hard work followed, but he conquered, and the place now comfortably sustains his own family and those of two sons. It is a wonder that so heavy a loss of hard-won earnings had not discouraged and broken him down, and ended his days. But his iron will conquered, and he went forth but the more determined to succeed. And now, after an absence of only a week, he longs for the quiet of his home again. Thither we are bound, as he tells the story. .

As we drove up through the Gap he told me how well he recollected when there was only a bridle-path through the Water Gap. The settlers above and below the Gap joined together and made the road. He had helped several days himself to build the road, besides subscribing money for this purpose.

At length we arrived at my own headquarters, and my guest sat down. He remained with me two days, and some of his reminiscences told me at that time I will now retell.

Joe Goodwin lived somewhere about Water Gap. He espoused the Indian cause, even to fighting with them against the whites. He liked the freedom of Indian life, and finally went off with them, leaving his relatives behind. His brother Isaac had a different taste, and the Indians had to keep out of reach of his well-aimed musket. Isaac said his brother was no better than an Indian, and that he had found his proper associates.

In time of the Indian troubles, Alaes Utt and a few others went out scouting for the "redskins." Walking along, he heard a gun fired, but still kept on his way. Presently he felt the blood trickling down under his clothes. Examining himself, he found he had been shot by some lurking Indian, the ball having passed entirely through, under his right arm, close to his body.. He felt the blood before he felt the shot. When the body is very hot from exercise or very cold from exposure, this is possible. Alaes went back, but the scout had found "game," and went on.

Mr. La Bar was acquainted with Goodwin, Alaes, and with Adam Utt, his brother. Adam was one of George's favorite chums. They were both great hunters, and long after the Indians had disappeared from this region, they have cabined in the woods, and hunted bear and deer for weeks in succession. Adam always carried a large wooden bowl and wooden spoon with him on his hunting expeditions, and a coffee-pot. He would make his coffee over the camp-fire, and pour it in his bowl, break up bread in it, and then sugar it, when his meal was ready. If he had brought down his buck, venison was toasted by the fire, and added to the savory meal.

Adam used to tell of a narrow escape from the Indians once on a time, near what is now called Spragueville. There were some half-a-dozen upon him before he knew it. Though not far from them when first discovered, he managed to dodge around through the laurels until, out of breath, he dropped behind a large rock, where, as they passed him in the search, he feared that they might hear the thumpings of his heart, which would not hold still. The rock that saved him still lies by the side of the road near the house of John Vanvliet. It was all woods there then.

At another time, Adam was out hunting on the "Cranberry Marsh," when he was attacked again by a large party of Indians. As they came up, he drew up his gun, and he saw one drop. He ran as far as his breath would carry him, and then hid in a thicket. They passed close by him, and he took an opposite direction and escaped.

CHAPTER XIV.

LIFE IN OLD TIMES.

Those good old times of long ago,
Ere Fashion reigned supreme,
When naught was done for pomp or show,
For less than it might seem.

MR. LA BAR began to keep house at first, as we have said, with his father-in-law. It was a log-house of one story. There were two rooms below, with a huge chimney, of stone, in the middle of the house. In the fireplace of the kitchen was a sort of iron box, or stove, which was walled into the fireplace in such a way as to open even with the back part of the fireplace, and then extended out into the room on the other side. It was like an iron oven, had no place for pipe, but the smoke came out where the wood was put in, and thence up the chimney with the smoke from the fireplace. This was the first idea of a stove. Buckwheat cakes were baked on this iron box in the opposite room from the kitchen; so we see buckwheat cakes were invented early. The father-in-law had wooden plates, but George adopted the new fashion and had earthen plates. Pewter was the improvement on these for the next generation, and crockery the one following.

A carpenter made a dresser, or cupboard, and a table for him, which are still in a good state of preservation, though upward of eighty years old. He had three or four splint-bottomed chairs, though benches were much in vogue.

The staple diet was mush and milk and potato-soup. Mills were too scarce for bread more than once a week — Sunday. Game was generally brought in also for this day, and then the tea was brought from the woods or the garden.

Women as well as men worked at clearing new ground and all out-door work. In fact, the women would work on the "farm" while the men went hunting or fishing. We see woman had many "rights" then. The wages for harvesting with the sickle was two shillings and sixpence, and women then had equal wages with men. This is the "right" claimed now of the "degenerated race." There are other rights "too tedious to mention."

Mr. La Bar was married in 1788, and in 1791 the Pennsylvania Whisky Insurrection broke out. There was great excitement, and the trouble became so alarming that the President called for the militia. George was wanted to fight the "whisky boys," but he had the camp fever. Dr. Larby attended him. The doctor lived where Major Lamb lived, at Portland.

He had been in the Revolution. Went west afterward, and died.

The doctor packed George in salt. (Is this what has preserved his old body so well?) As soon as he could stand alone he went to Richmond to attend the appeal, where he was honorably excused.

The "house tax" followed in 1798 as the next trouble. The excitement in Mount Bethel exceeded the whisky trouble. There was a very general resistance to the law throughout the whole county. It was a direct tax of the United States, and was levied on the number of windows, or the size and number of the panes of glass in the houses. The people took it as they had taken the British duty on tea, as an imposition and wrong. The assessors were boldly forbidden to act, under threats of personal violence. Men armed themselves to resist the hated law. One John Fries made himself conspicuous as a leader of the insurgents. But the difficulty was at length crushed. Fries was arrested for treason, found guilty, and sentenced to be hung, but was afterward pardoned by President Adams. Several others were found guilty of treason in a lesser degree, and spent terms in prison, when general quiet was again restored. George still lived with his father-in-law at this time. The house had two windows, and he paid one dollar tax. It was paid in "stamp paper." Jacob Utt and Ed. Lowery were assessor and collector in that place. They did not try to collect the tax above the mountain.

Mr. La Bar remembers very distinctly General Sullivan's march to Wilkesbarre and farther up the Susquehanna. General Sullivan started from Easton in 1779, to clear out the Indians from the frontier. He crossed the Blue Ridge through Wind Gap, cutting the road for his army. This road has been used ever since, having been changed very little from the old route.

The Pennsylvanians as early as 1793 began to see the necessity of some better communication with the settlements in the west end of the State, and with Ohio.

The Whisky Rebellion was incited by the difficulty of pack-horse transportation. A farmer in Pittsburg could not by this means afford to carry wheat to Philadelphia, but he *could* make it into whisky, when one horse could carry twenty-four bushels in alcohol. The tax touched their only means of exchange, and the farther west the more severely the effect was felt and shown. The canal question was agitated; several companies were organized; some short lines opened, and, in 1825, the work was begun, when, in a few years, a way was opened to the Ohio River, and pack-horse communication had had its day. The time soon followed when the canal was too slow for Yankee enterprise and progress.

Mr. La Bar being at Easton, one day when General Washington was soon expected to visit that place, resolved to wait and see the Father of his Country. As the expected hour drew near, every flag in the place was flung to the breeze; all the military of that region assembled to do honor to the man; the cannons were loaded and primed, ready for a salute; the fifes and drums that had marshaled some of the same soldiers on the battle-fields of the Revolution, were waiting to strike joyful notes of welcome.

At length, the little company of horsemen is seen coming in the distance. The cannons belch forth their harmless wads, and shake the earth as best they can, for that early day. The fife and drum keep silence no longer, while the glad populace ring out cheer after cheer.

They enter the little town, and the joy and gladness is unbounded. It is no difficult matter to distinguish the loved and honored guest. Tall, commanding, majestic, he sits on his white charger, "the noblest work of God." Were he not a *man*, he would be a king. But the man is superior to the king — stately, graceful, honoring, honored. Following him, on a black horse, is his black servant, whose life is so wrapped up in a faithful service to his faithful master that, in studying to anticipate his wants, he barely notices what is going on around him.

George Washington alights, and after the soldiers, the citizens take him by the hand. George shared the privilege of touching the great and good man, and was satisfied as he turned to his team, and was soon on his way homeward.

The war of 1812 followed. Mr. La Bar now lived on his own place at Slateford. The call was for men between the ages of twenty-one and forty-five. He was then forty-nine: had been just too young for the Revolution, was too old for 1812! He had a boy almost twenty-one years old. The Revolution had been a success when the whole population of the Colonies was about what that of the city of New York is to-day, and no one doubted the issue of 1812. Everybody was confident of success, and there were no Tories to be found. This confidence allayed excitement, and the war went on as any man would now go forward with a large contract. The fighting-ground did not reach Pennsylvania, and business went forward unchecked during the war. Afterward there was a "tightness" followed, which affected the financial affairs of States and individuals. Specie almost disappeared, and paper became quite

worthless.   But the end came at last, and
prosperity and progress went onward.

The two-days' visit ended.   I suggested to
my guest that it would be more comfort-
able for him to accompany me to Spragueville
on the cars, and from thence, three miles, by
carriage to his house.   He declined riding in
the cars.   He said he had got along so far in his
life by walking or riding behind oxen or horses,
that he had made up his mind not to put on
steam now.   I still tried to prevail on him to
try the cars "just once," but he said he wanted
to see the road as he passed, and to have the
reins close to him.   I accepted the argument,
and the carriage conveyed him safely back to his
dear old home.

CHAPTER XV.

RELIGION AND POLITICS.

All men, no matter what their state,
Of the Supreme are taught innate:
First God, their family, and then
Their country—these the truest men.

TOWARD the close of February, 1870, I
went to visit my old friend again. I
found him enjoying excellent health, and appa-
rently in better condition than when I saw him
in September. He recognized me at once, and
there was no need of caution and reserve.
There had been much sickness in that vicinity
during the winter, but he, like an old, gnarled
oak, had stood unscathed through all the unusual changes of the season. His eye was
bright and clear, his frame so steady and elastic
that he used no cane while around the house
or near the door. He is the wonder of himself and all that see him. I have seen men of
sixty, who exhibited more of the second childhood than he. He chops a little wood at the
door occasionally, and has been on the point
of going to the woods to get out railroad ties
this winter, but a sudden change of weather
has prevented thus far. His eye looks so clear
that I suppose a skillful optician could fit

him with glasses with which he could see quite
as well as ever; but then he cannot read, and
he can see well enough for his purpose. He
has a sturdy appetite, and nothing disarranges
his stomach. He can eat anything any one
can, but molasses is, and always has been, a
staple part of his diet. Coffee and tea he has
always used since these have been used in old
Northampton. He still chews tobacco, as he
always has, and his pipe is not neglected. He
trembles very little under his load of years, and
helps himself at the table as usual. He talks
frequently of the God in whom he trusts. His
faith is of the strongest character, reminding
me of the patriarchs of Old Testament days.

The blessing I heard him ask at his own
table, I will here repeat:

"Our Father in heaven, we thank Thee for
this nourishment, provided for our weak and
decaying bodies. Keep us from all evil. When
done with us in this life, take us to dwell with
Thee, for our Lord Jesus Christ's sake. Amen."
After this, and in a lower tone, he said, "Lord,
be with me this day."

Mr. La Bar made no profession of religion
until about twenty-six years ago. He was
converted during a revival, under the preach-
ing of Rev. —— Cullen, and was immersed by
him, with some twenty others, in Marshall's
Creek. He believed he was soundly converted,

and he has continued in the faith. Stalbert preached in that vicinity about the same time. The nearest church is some three miles distant, and an appointment was made at the school-house close by. That good old veteran, Father Barrass, preached at this school-house every four weeks, for many years, until, last fall, he went to his reward. Grandfather La Bar has heard no sermons since.

To illustrate the faith I have referred to, I will relate an incident which Mr. La Bar told me with that childlike earnestness which disperses all doubt.

About twenty years ago, there was a very great drought in this vicinity. It was in the latter part of the summer, and the corn was wilted and drooping; the buckwheat stood scorched and shrivelled. Even the leaves on the trees were, in some places, curling up and paling. He had been contemplating the parched scene, when, thinking of patriarchal prevalence in prayer, he resolved to pray for rain. He got on his knees, in the open air, and prayed long and earnestly for the desired rain. Rising to his feet, he looked around and saw the scene unchanged. He fell down and prayed again; rose up, and yet no sign. He knelt and prayed yet again with all the fervency of his heart and the fullest faith. When he rose up, he looked for the expected cloud, and behold, it had risen! The blessed shower was coming; his prayer had been answered. Before he reached his house, the thirsty earth was drinking in the refreshing draught.

The shower lasted long, and was plenteous. The old man's heart was so grateful that he could scarcely contain himself. He told his family he had prayed for the rain, and his prayers were answered. The shower continuing long, one of his boys thought there was more than enough, and asked the old man why he did not pray for the rain to stop? The old man told him *he* might do that.

Now we will go back again to Hunter's settlement. The first voting-place for Mount Bethel was at Richmond. There Mr. La Bar voted for the first President of the United States, George Washington. *He has voted at every Presidential election since that time*, either in Northampton County or in Monroe, which was cut off the former in 1834. He has never lived outside the bounds of the original county in which he was born. It has been said that Northampton was chopped in two in order to suit the necessity of the rapidly expanding family of La Bars, who could see no better way to make two families of them than by stringing the Blue Ridge between them.

But to the voting. George has always voted the Democratic ticket, and rather glories in the fact. He says, if there has been a change of base, it is not his fault. He has followed the true meaning of the word democracy, and that he considers good enough for an American citizen. But where is there another man living who has voted every time a President has been chosen since this has been a Republic?

The first meeting-house erected north of Brainerd's Bethel Church was the old log-house at Williamsburg. Another was built soon after at Richmond, *alias* Rum Corner. Rum and religion, very frequently, went hand in hand in those days. The tavern and the church were early necessities, and were often planted side by side. A preacher who did not drink rum was an exception; and no wonder, when every family was more careful to keep their rum-jug full than their jug for molasses. The head of the family would fill the glass before breakfast, sweeten it to the taste of the children, pass it round to young and old, and then they were ready for the morning meal. The bad custom was so general that few suspected the evil. Mathews, Neimigher, and Clinkins were the earliest preachers of the vicinity.

Most of the early settlers had come to this country on account of religious persecution; but the religion they brought with them was not over-zealous when opposition ceased.

7

Under the circumstances, we would have supposed that the religious liberty now enjoyed
would have burned in their hearts, and led each
to a height of Christian love and ardor never exhibited to the world before. But it was not so.
Their religion was cold and formal, and only
grew as a stunted tree transplanted into an un-
fruitful soil. It did seem as though persecution
was necessary to a lively growth of religion.
The day of sacrifice was past, and with it their
best joy.

The first school-house erected in the north-
ern part of Mount Bethel was at Dill's Ferry,
about where the tannery now is. It was a
side-light that did not reflect far, but it was the
beginning of better days.

The first grist-mill was erected by Henry
Forgeman. It stood about half a mile west
of Williamsburg. Forgeman moved West soon
after the Revolution; and some years after, his
son, William, with his wife, came from Ohio,
all the way on horseback, to visit their old
friends in Mount Bethel.

The first store was at Williamsburg, by Jake
Detrich; but store-keeping did not amount to
much then. Molasses, salt, and sugar had to
be bought at the store, but the people could
make their own clothing, rye-coffee, mush and
milk, and spice-wood tea.

After the township became divided, Williamsburg became the voting-place, and a tavern appeared to meet the necessity!

Moses Tatamy, an old Indian-hunter, had a cabin and lived close at the foot of the mountain at Tat's Gap, and thus the name that notch has always retained.

The Indian name of Brodhead's Creek was Analomink, and this name it should have retained; though, next to that, its present name should have the preference, as Daniel Brodhead was the first settler who purchased land bounded by the creek for any considerable distance. His tract reached from somewhere near Experiment Mills, on the north side, to a point near Spragueville. He settled there in 1737.

Marshall's Creek was named after the noted pedestrian of the Indian Walk, Edward Marshall.

McMichael's Creek was named after an early squatter, who was in bad repute with both whites and Indians here.

Pocono Creek retains its proper Indian name, which Cherry Creek failed to do.

CHAPTER XVI.

THE COMPARISON.

Days come and go in constant flow —
With noiseless steppings glide —
But bars will shift and wash and drift
Before the moving tide ;
So when these days to years have run,
To centuries, see we what is done.

WE have been looking upon a man, still living, who had an existence when this part of Pennsylvania was the frontier, and the Indians were just about leaving this vicinity never to return. The war of the Revolution hurried on, bringing its burden of trial and trouble; but joy followed, for a new nation was born, the greatness of which none had faith enough to picture. This, too, sank into the past. Intestine difficulties rose and subsided. The new Government, adjusting itself to circumstances, grew in strength and power. A grand Republic, established more as an experiment than to be a reality, was becoming a successful fact. Improvement and resources were developing, and the nineteenth century dawned.

Then succeeded the war of 1812, with all the train of ills peculiar to this mode of settling difficulties between nations — and this, too, passed by.

Another decade, and enterprise and progress went on anew. Men were beginning to live and do. Books were multiplied, and the arts and sciences advanced. Steam, as a working helper, was introduced. Communication by canal and turnpikes and other means of transportation were showing important results.

Yet another decade, and the locomotive began its mighty revolution and revelation. Civilization now took wonderful strides. The American Nation was reaching up to the level of the most enlightened and prosperous nations of the earth. Common schools and schools uncommon reached out to do good to all, and to spread the light.

Another ten years, and the telegraph was born from the brain of an American. Steam-ship communication brought far-off countries comparatively nigh. Commerce reached out to all the chief ports of the earth. The war with Mexico was but the brushing away of an annoying fly.

When half the century had passed, we were a great nation, of great wealth and enterprise. From about one million in 1763, now we numbered about twenty-three millions of earnest, intelligent, wide-awake people. Books and periodicals flooded the land with light for the

eyes and food for the mind. The great valley
of the Mississippi is dotted with a busy population from its source to its mouth. From the
Eastern States to that valley is one broad, cultivated field, thickly interspersed with thriving
towns and cities. And still

"Westward the star of empire takes its way."

The magic picture is still changing and expanding, year after year, and the motto is "Onward."

Another decade, and the tide of prosperity
had been unchecked, but soon the war-trump
sounded again. Vast armies responded, un-
paralleled in numbers by anything seen in
modern times, and the grandchildren of those
who had fought side by side in the Revolution
and in the war of 1812, were now arrayed in
mortal combat against each other. It was a
sickening picture; but the "accursed thing"
was found upon us, and this was the means
an overruling Providence ordered upon us to
root out the evil. Those terrible scenes passed
on and were numbered with the past, though
their memory is so fresh in the minds of millions.

And now the "numbering year" has come
again. The telegraph lies at the bottom of the
broad Atlantic, while from continent to continent the thought-current talks intelligently and
outstripping time. Upon the land the vast
network reaches to the most secluded part of

civilization.   Across the continent, and up and down, here and there and everywhere the iron-horse dashes away, developing and unfolding the greatness of this Great Land.   And how many are we to-day — forty millions?   Onward, onward!

All these stirring events, a living panorama, unpainted, seen, felt, experienced in a human life which still runs on!   Wonderful, wonderful!   Who can realize such a mighty sweep of real revelations?   Two centuries and three quarters had passed since the discovery of America, and but little benefit had, as yet, accrued to the human family; but in the last one hundred and six years there has been a great making-up for all those previous years.

CHAPTER XVII.

NUMBERS.

"Be fruitful, and multiply, and replenish the earth, and sub-due it."

THE La Bar stock, commingling with the German, have well obeyed the injunction to Adam and Eve, and have shown a prolific family. The three pioneer French brothers now show a living progeny of about seven thousand two hundred! We have based our calculations on a seven-fold ratio of increase to obtain this number in four generations.

If we take the family of Mr. George La Bar as a rule for the rest, we find he has ten children who have raised families, and his grand-children number about eighty. Now here is a ten-fold increase, after we throw away eight children as non-producing. He has a son who has about the same number of grandchildren. Mr. La Bar has had fourteen children in all. But, if we throw away three-sevenths for death and casualties, we will have four-sevenths, or eight of the fourteen left, as producing mem-bers. He had ten such, but we will make eight the producing stock, and the result will show an army of twelve thousand two hundred and seventy. This may be too high, but we should remember that we have been counting but four generations, whereas there have been at least five generations since the original brothers went out from their bachelor cabin.

Again, George's eight producing children increased by a ratio of eight, and we have sixty-four grandchildren; then throwing away the three-sevenths, we have four-sevenths, or thirty-seven left, which, increased again by our ratio, we have two hundred and ninety-six great-grandchildren. Deducting and multiplying as before, we have thirteen hundred and sixty great-great-grandchildren, most of them yet to be!

Of course, one-half of the La Bar descendants have many different names, coming from the female side, which is changed by marriage. I find the La Bar blood reaches into almost every family in Mount Bethel and Monroe County, and across the river into Warren County, New Jersey.

George La Bar's oldest child was born in 1791, and is therefore seventy-nine years of age. He was married at twenty-one to a girl of thirteen. *Their* oldest child is now fifty-six. This is Mr. La Bar's oldest grandchild. The old son and his young wife are still living, having raised a large family. So it seems to be healthy for a girl to marry at thirteen.

Their oldest child is less than fifteen years younger than his mother, and his head is far whiter to-day than his old grandfather of one hundred and seven years.

George La Bar is perhaps the oldest man in Pennsylvania. We have seen the hardy character of his progenitors — that they were men and women always used to hardship, toil, and danger. Their food was of the simplest kind, and eaten to sustain life rather than to pamper. Their clothing was neither broadcloth, beaver, nor silk. Their cabins were always well ventilated, and the open fireplace, with the "backlog" always burning, like an inverted funnel, sucked the fresh air through every crack between the chinked logs.

The grandfather and his two brothers brought with them their mother tongue, with a fair share of French politeness and education, but these soon wore out before the more prevalent language of the men of the forest, and of the German settlers following, with whom they associated, and of whom they married. Politeness does not so grow into the bone and marrow of even a Frenchman but that it can become blunted by the adverse circumstances of a frontier life.

Then, again, here were foreigners, coming to a new country, and joining hands and hearts. The first union was French and German, and then it was a mixture of American-born with most of the German element. Finally, after a few generations, both dropped the original languages brought over the water, and adopted the English. All the descendants produced large families, and they have, generally, lived to a ripe old age.

Now there is much written and said about "sanitary affairs," and a thousand "helps" are given to obtain a long life. One learned man has one hobby, and another has another, for the same object. My experience is that every person should be so well acquainted with himself and his own system and nature, that he can choose for himself what is best for his own health, better than any one outside of that system, though he be the wisest M. D. that ever lived. How far this wisdom can carry us into the years to come, we know not. If we fail, the mistake will be upon us, and not in the mistake of a hired operator. Mr. La Bar was an unlearned man, and yet his instinctive taste chose well for him, and no philosophy ever led him to turn away from what nature asked in the way of taste and appetite.

CHAPTER XVIII.

CONCLUSION.

The aged pilgrim, as he stands
    And waits the parting wave,
Looks over Jordan to that land
    Of bliss beyond the grave;
Then with a longing heart he treads,
    As forth the pillar moves,
And the cold stream no longer dreads,
    To reach the God he loves.

MR. LA BAR has always been of a quiet, contented disposition, avoiding strife and contention, not easily excited, choosing to bear rather than resent. He always recognized a Supreme Being and an over-ruling Providence, although he did not dedicate himself to the service of Heaven until he was eighty years of age. Since that time his life has been of the firmest trust and confidence in God, even experiencing in his own daily life that "all things work together for good to them that walk uprightly." Long waiting, it has always been with "Thy will be done," and without one lurking doubt of his acceptance. Trust—this it is that affords him that blessed peace of mind which enables him to look forward complacently, feeling that all is well, for he knows in Whom he believes. Death has no terrors, for as Jordan parted when the ark of the covenant moved forward, o'er-shadowed by the pillar of cloud which gave the signal to go over, so he waits the beckoning of the angels, yet satisfied to wait.

That waiting may continue for years, even yet; for his health is good, and there is no indication of an early breaking down of that strong body, which has borne up so wonderfully under one hundred and seven years. He sleeps well, and rises early, as he always has been in the habit of doing. His mind is clear, and shows less of the "second childhood" than I have seen in some persons of sixty years. He says he has only turned back to the small figures, to go up the scale of boyhood again, and that he will soon be old enough to go to school. He is not troubled much with aches and pains, is contented and cheerful, enjoys life as well as ever. He is not a burden to any one, and never has been.

What I consider as the most remarkable thing in Mr. La Bar's history, is the fact that he has never given up keeping his own house and his own table. He is of too independent a character to permit himself to become a dependent on his children, or any of their descendants, so long as he is able to have it otherwise. He is still "master of the situation," and competent to rule his own house.

Most aged persons give up when they find their life-partner gone, but not so with him. His wife has been dead some thirty years, and all their children had gone out to do for themselves many years before.

Before I became much acquainted with the family, I asked Mr. La Bar if he had been married more than once. He said he had not; that he had had a good wife once, and, though tempted to marry again, he feared he might get a devil, and did not make the venture. I was satisfied with the answer.

He says that though but a boy, he bore his part of the trouble of the Revolution, felt the anxieties of the Whisky Rebellion, and the riot of the house-tax; passed the trying times that followed the war of 1812, and bore his part toward paying its debt; and, at last, after living through the Great Rebellion, he thinks this last "bounty tax" has nothing to do with him, and says he so told the collector. The collector said he would excuse him "next time." Uncle George thinks he will hardly wait to see another "onpleasantness" settled by the sword.

Besides the young sister, aged eighty-six, spoken of before, Mr. La Bar has another sister living, aged about ninety-two, and a brother, living in Canada, who is about ninety-eight. This brother was down on a visit to George about two years ago. He is a smart old lad, too.

He presented George with a silver-mounted cane, which is highly prized, more especially for the giver's sake than for its real necessity to him.

And now the "tale is told," and yet not all told, for the sands are still dropping, dropping, and the end is yet to come. Of that busy life which has numbered so many years, it is but the merest fraction of a whole that has had the slightest notice by my pen. Only in the great Judgment Day can the one hundred and seven volumes, of three hundred and sixty-five pages each, be read entire! No thought, no word, no action, has been lost; all have been recorded! When we take into consideration the restless activity of the mind; the perpetual throbbings of the human heart; the constant heaving and contraction of the chest,; the hundreds of muscles brought into exercise with every step we take, every action we perform; the unceasing wear and repair — our wonder grows into amazement that so frail a body should ever be found to live to the *one hundred and seventh year!*

www.ingramcontent.com/pod-product-compliance
Lightning Source LLC
Chambersburg PA
CBHW032147010726
47493CB00008BA/2612